The Simple Things

Jannicke Howard

Copyright © Louise Clark 2004
This edition 2009
All rights reserved. No part of this book may be used or reproduced in any manner whatsoever without the written permission of the copyright owner.
Cover art and design copyright © Louise Clark 2009

Published using Lulu.com
ISBN 978-0-9559923-2-2

In a fit of fury, Aran Sellere had flushed all of his antidepressants down the toilet last night. He had been feeling particularly frustrated by the way things had worked out and had come to the conclusion that downing a timetable of pills and talking his colleagues and associates into believing he was going to make a come back was not the way to sort out his life.

Something bigger was needed. He was leaving.

He sat and watched his old editor talking. The way that big mouth swilled round; the red wine-stained teeth in the grimy hole. It reminded him of his pills being sucked down into the London sewerage system.

In turn, the editor watched Aran as he talked, and though it was a real tragedy to see talent go this way. Everyone had their peak, but they didn't necessarily have to crash so apocalypticly afterwards.

Aran had been an excellent investigative reporter. He'd originally started out as a local rag photographer and built up his career from there. He had moved down to London to work on the nationals. At the top of his game, he had been freelance, contributing to all the nationals, the big international magazines, Christ, there had even been talk of books in the near future. He really had it all.

It was at that point that things had started to go wrong. Where as most people tended to fade away, sometimes even keeping the distinguished connotations to their name, Aran seemed to be going for total annihilation of reputation.

"I bumped into Geoffrey the other day," he told Aran. "He told me you said you were going to write the Knight biography." It was always possible that Geoffrey had misheard the pitch. Or that this was an elaborate joke, although he could think of no reason why anyone could be so cruel.

Aran, a man once dignified, now dropping off into incoherent tramp territory, slouched somewhat ungraciously in the chair on the opposing side of the desk. It didn't look as though he had cut his hair for a few months. The stubble was creeping onto beard. Judging by the way the jumper hung, it looked as though he had lost a bit of weight. Everyone had heard that old theory of untidiness being a sign of creativity, but this really was trying too hard.

"Geoffrey's always trying to over dramatise his own dull little existence," Aran responded. "Besides, someone will eventually do the Patrick Knight biography. No one believes that feeble statement he gave announcing retirement. The man's only fifty for Christ's sake."

"I'm not disputing that." He sat up a little straighter, sighing inwardly that he would have to play father figure. Someone needed to get Aran back on track. People in the profession said it had been triggered by that badly handled report on missing teenagers – a melodramatic shocker at best. Friends said the cracks had been appearing before then. "I had one guy from the office working on a similar story. No one got anywhere near Knight. It's been over a year now. The man's locked himself in that big country mansion. Mission accomplished."

Aran just shrugged.

The editor rolled his yes. No mortal man was ever going to get an exclusive out of Patrick Knight. Not even Aran Sellere, as mad as he was.

"The point is," the editor started, still watching for signs of a breaking smile to signify the wind up. "Everyone else is getting realistic. No one's going to get it out of him. Whatever plausible theory happens to be right. The man's ill, he's disillusioned with life… I don't know; he wants to live alone in the rain and write his bloody memoirs. There is a story, but no one's going to get it. We all know how determined he is. Every sodding trick has been tried, believe me, I've had every hack coming in here with no end of ridiculous suggestions. You haven't even got a plan."

Aran scowled. "Have I said to you that I'm going to write the biography? I still don't know why you dragged me up here for a bloody meeting. You don't appear to have any work for me. I'm not some board room suit; I am a journalist." Say it enough times and someone might believe you.

"Yeah, you were a damn good one!" The editor shook a fist full of papers at him. "Until that bloody article about missing teenagers. I thought it was going to be bloody human interest. A twist on the old story how ordinary people go missing every other day. But what you somehow, and god only knows how, managed to get into my paper was sensationalist melodrama. You'd have been better off reporting on Elvis sightings for crying out loud. So what does this tell you?"

"You think this is a load of bollocks?"

"Damn right. I sincerely hope you're not planning on wasting your time trying to get to the Knight story. Everything's been tried. Patrick Knight is keeping stum. You can say all you like that you think there's something sinister going on, which there most probably isn't, but you're not getting a word of it in print. You are wasting your time."

Aran leant forward to the desk. "Knight is not perfect. No one is. There must be something."

The editor smiled without humour. "I thought you weren't doing the story."

"I'm not."

Silence settled between them; a thin layer of dusty stalemate. The editor stared at him, almost horrified at his persistence. "Something, yeah, there must be something," he nodded slowly. "There's never been a politician more liked than Knight. Can't do a thing wrong. A contradiction in terms. Too much so for it to just be good PR. His reasons for abruptly quitting political and public life are probably just so boring that he's embarrassed to say. He just wants to get out of it all. Which incidentally is what I think you should do. Stop looking for your come back story. Just stop for a while and get your head sorted." It was hard to know what more to say. "You have a really good reputation. I know things have been a bit slack the past year or so, but even so. Look, I've heard you've been having a few problems…"

"That's irrelevant."

"All right, it's irrelevant," he sighed. "You want my advice? Take a break. Just get away and take a holiday, forget about writing for a few months."

Aran stood up. "Why did you drag me down here?"

"Professional concern."

There was little point in arguing further. It wouldn't change anything. Perhaps with a couple of days to consider the issue, he would find his sanity and get back to the good journalism he was known for. So what if it had been a quiet year? Never mind that god-awful article. We were all allowed one disaster. But there were very strict rules on repeat offenders.

"What are you going to do?"

Aran didn't answer immediately, staring out of the window onto London. "I've got a few things to tie up with the move. I think I'm going to get out of the city."

"Yeah." The editor slumped in defeat, watching as Aran pulled open the office door. "You think about what I said."

She had smiled lightly and shrugged. "It's just one of those things."

He supposed it was just one of those things; running his hand down the length of the kitchen table. He had known the day he met her in the rain in Hyde Park that she was one of those women. She had never lied as such about her nature. Just avoided the issue, skipped around the consequences. Relationships never really ended; she gradually drifted out of one as a new man appeared in her life. He hadn't realised that his time too had come to an end.

"I can't believe you're just up and leaving."

Aran looked up from examining the grain of the wood. Two years he had sat here every morning and eaten breakfast. Two years they had lived together, only a couple of months after meeting. Now she was already settled in a new relationship, with an upwardly mobile banker and a spacious Georgian town house. She had finally broken the news a month ago and left him with a flat he couldn't afford.

"You know as well as I do that I can't afford the rent on this place on my own."

The other man in the kitchen nodded, leaning against the tall freezer and stuffing his hands into his pockets. He felt like a vulture, picking off the remains. "Haven't thought about getting a lodger?"

Aran snorted at the suggestion. "I've had enough of all that."

"I suppose so," he sighed, looking back to the table and imagining how it would look in his own new flat. "And as friends we've got to take advantage of the situation," he added lightly, trying to soothe his conscience with a joke. "You're sure you're not going to change your mind?"

"No," he was quite definite on that point. "Take the table. I want to sell off everything, make a clean start of it."

The flat was a hollow shell; a few pieces scattered like frightened animals at the edges of rooms. Essential personal belongings boxed up, some already in storage. The new tenants were moving in next week.

"What are your plans, then?" the man asked, watching Aran cautiously, half expecting him to break down. "You taking a holiday?"

"Not really," Aran answered, slouching on the window sill. "I am getting out of the city though. I don't know if I'll be back, permanently, I mean. I need a bit of time to try and sort my life out, decide what's next."

"And you're not going to be working for a bit?"

Aran looked up sharply. "That's a leading question. Who've you been talking to?"

"No one."

"I don't believe you."

"Really."

Silence.

"All right, so I happened to hear from Paul."

"Come off it, no one ever happens to hear from Paul."

"He sounded a bit worried about you, which was a surprise considering it was Paul," the man confessed. "He wouldn't say what it was exactly, just that you were planning a new story. A waste of time that might land you in trouble if you try too hard."

"Well, that's his opinion."

"Seriously. He seemed to think it could do your reputation irreparable damage. You're not still going ahead with it are you?"

There was no answer. He watched Aran jangle his keys around on his finger. The past month had not been good. Some people had even been worried before Melissa announced the split and walked out. Aran's career seemed to be drying up; perhaps there was no more reachable injustice left for him to protest about. He'd been going through a creative blip. A blip that had finished with an embarrassing article charting the disappearance of some teenagers from the north in melodramatic fashion worthy of any romantic housewife's novel. Now one of his few constants had walked out on him in an unsettlingly casual manner, and he had slipped into deep brooding. Nuances of paranoia. It was hard to keep a conversation going with him for any length of time. Everyone said he needed to get away for a while, before hen completely fell to pieces. Pull yourself right out of the situation and try to remember who it was exactly that you were supposed to be.

"I've let the property agents know you've bought the table, that you'll be picking it up later in the week," Aran spoke, changing the subject with a sharp reverse. "Just give the woman a call and fix a time."

"You're not going to be here?"

Aran shook his head. "I'm heading up north tomorrow."

"Whereabouts?"

"Just a little place out in the middle of nowhere. I'm going to rent a cottage for a few months; decide where to go from there."

"Right," the man hovered awkwardly in the doorway. He had outstayed what little welcome there had been. "I'd better be off. Think about what Paul said."

Aran grimaced and looked out of the window. There was little else to do but think. Think about the misery people inflicted on others. Think about his life, the few shreds that were left. Think, and think again. And when the doctor told you that you were thinking the wrong kind of thoughts, there was always medication to take. Aran had robotically taken the pills for a couple of weeks, then decided it was hardly a solution to his life. He knew from the glances, the awkward hushes and the side stepping that people thought he was on the verge of a mental break down. Aran Sellere was no longer the writer he had once been.

He would pull himself out of this hole, he promised as he pocketed the keys. He would come back with gut wrenching impact and show them all.

In dusky summer light, as evening pulled closer, a car slowed into the only available parking slot in front of the *Fox and Hound*. Silence swelled upon the vehicle again: the pure, unpolluted soundlessness of the deep countryside. It was a sharply different world to the one he had become lost within, the mass urban sprawl of London.

Aran kept his hands on the steering wheel after the engine had stopped as if afraid to let go. He looked out at the surroundings he would be considering home for the next few months. This was his new local: the *Fox and Hound*. It was the embodiment of everything the tourist brochures promised: hanging baskets of brightly coloured perennials that lined the front of the pub; the long selection of local ales; the down to earth chatter drifting along the bar. It was also the address he had been given to collect the keys.

He had been looking for somewhere away from large populated areas to come and re cooperate. This area had appealed and it was selected – the fact that it was in close proximity to Knight's estate a complete coincidence, he told himself, for he had not even decided definitely if he would bother with the biography.

Aran had rung around various self-catering options and short term tenancies and eventually managed to find a suitably priced cottage. He had been lucky, it was July and most places were booked up for the holiday season; the tenancies not coming up as no one wanted to think about getting new lodgers.

One farmer's wife had been able to help after a brief telephone conversation and a lot of procrastinating. There had to be somewhere he could stay at a relatively cheap price. All of her holiday cottages were fully booked, but when she understood his situation and the fact that he was prepared to take anything, she mentioned a run down cottage a mile or so out of the village. They were slowly renovating it, and it was habitable, but in no state to be put in the tourist brochures, what with the outdoor lavatory and a great lack of modern kitchen conveniences. Yet she would be willing to let him stay there for a small price for a few months if he was prepared to take it as it came. He had accepted before she had chance to retract her uncertain offer, and had quickly scribbled down the address before hurrying away to pack his car.

His instructions were to pick up the keys from the landlady of the *Fox and Hound*. The owner of the cottage, the farmer's wife, was away for a week visiting her sister in Cornwall. The pub was easy enough to find, as all centres of alcohol uncannily seem to be; but the cottage could be easily missed. Apparently it was easy to loose your sense of direction. Blends of narrow farm roads, randomly lurching up on foreign motorists, twisting through the hill country; the distinct lack of signposts; natural landmarks that looked like the previous one.

Aran took a moment to stretch his legs after the long drive before entering the pub. Behind the bricks and mortar was the faded sound of lively chatter. Over a low fence he could see groups of people sat outside in the beer garden, talking and laughing over a pint before they would wander home. Inviting, open, yet he felt excluded by it, the stranger in the evening. No one noticed his arrival.

Pushing open the door, he slipped into the noisy bar as if invisible. Within large groups of people he frequently vanished with ease. It was not to say that he was a dull creature unworthy of notice. His sense of self and his thoughts ran deep, and even on the most superficial of levels he had always been considered somewhat attractive, if in a careless way. More that he was quiet by nature, traversing through crowds as if a ghost. Advantageous in his profession. He slipped into conferences, parties and meetings he really had no right to attend. A fellow journalist had once asked him for a quote as he had marched out of a science conference. Conversations that were technically private, property trespassed; secrets picked out and at the end of the day when the papers had the facts in print, people could not really recall if there had been a man there they didn't know. Quiet and confident, more often than not people presumed he had every right to enter.

A large woman with curly brown hair stood behind the bar. She had an empty beer glass in her hand as she turned around to face her public. She locked eyes with the stranger; he carefully slipping past a group of cackling farmers who had become a little too merry on the cider this evening. He was a curiosity, and something new at the bar was always welcome.

"I'm looking for the landlady,"

"And you've found her, darling," she responded, her bright red lips glittering. She leant brazenly across the bar. Her eyes still bore into him, desperate to know who he was. "Let me guess," she continued as he opened his mouth to say something. "You must be Aran Sellere."

He smiled, only with the mouth, but it was still a smile. "Yes. I was told I could pick the keys to the cottage up from here."

"Indeed you can. I'm Adele Witherspoon, nice to meet you. Betty has a spare set here as well as a map. I'll just get them."

A scrawny, balding man with moustache staggered out into the bar walkway as if he had just tripped over something. Adele trotted past on her high heels, barely noticing him.

"It's a bloody filthy mess back there, you know," he grumbled irritably. "I don't see why she can't come Tuesdays as well."

Adele patted him on the shoulder with little concern. Fixture and fittings. She always knew when he was there. Didn't even have to look. "Yes, Bill," she sighed as if she had heard this many times before. "I tell you, we want Ludvine back."

"Yes, well, we can't have everything, now can we?" he commented flatly as he looked across the bar, reading the lay of drinks and settling on a figure that stood drinkless. "I'm sorry sir, has my wife not served you yet?"

Aran shook his head. "I'm just here to pick up the keys to the cottage."

"But you'll stay and have a drink, will you not?" Bill questioned, eager to make another sale as he set himself by the beer pump.

"Not tonight. I've had a long drive. I just want to get some sleep."

"We'll say another night, then," Bill spoke as if he was going to hold Aran to it on pain of death. "Ay, Betty mentioned you; Aran Sellere, wasn't it? You're staying for a few months in that old run down cottage. By, you must be desperate if you're staying there. Of course it's habitable," he quickly added. "And it does have some very impressive views. It's just a bit basic, you might say."

"That really doesn't bother me."

"And you say you had a long drive. Where do you come from, then?" Bill was keen to make conversation. Talking was something that both he and his wife lived for; there was previous little else to do. Tourists, passers by, anyone with a willing face were all treated the same.

"I drove up from London."

"London, eh? You don't sound like a southerner."

"I'm not," Aran responded, wishing Adele would hurry up with the keys. "I'm actually from the Shetlands."

Bill raised his eyebrows as if not quite convinced.

"I've moved around a lot."

He nodded. "It happens these days."

"Here you are, darling." Adele bustled back with a bunch of keys and a crisp, photocopied hand drawn map. "Keys to the cottage and a map to get you there."

"He doesn't need that," Bill grunted, a firm and misguided believer in the male ability to cope without maps and instruction manuals. "You saw the two hills behind the pub? You want to follow the road that goes between them. A mile or so and you'll come to a little dirt track going off to the left. There's one of those old fashioned post boxes still dangling on the fence, little more than a rusty tin can now, but you'll recognise it when you see it. Can't miss it."

"Right, thanks." Aran accepted the keys and the map. "I'll probably see you again whilst I'm up here."

"That we will," Bill agreed. "We are your local by miles."

He would be back at the pub. If nothing else it would be a rich source of local gossip and legend, one method of harvesting background details. For that biography he probably wasn't going to write.

He reversed smoothly out of the parking space and swung onto the main road. Main was an overstatement, but in comparison to the surroundings, this minor road was the lifeline pumping through the sparsely populated area.

It was dark, but not dark enough for the surrounding countryside to disappear. The moon was full and clear of any cloud cover. Cold ivory light streamed out to touch upon the landscape. The temperature dropped as he followed the road through the flat valley between the two hills. For the first time that summer, he visibly shivered.

He peered out of his car with the look nearing that of a dazed creature as he drove past a long grazing field. Details out of the windscreen so clear as if they had been magnified. The field was fenced off and currently empty of livestock; a windblown plain of thick grass at the foot of the small hill. Out in the far centre of the field, a figure stood.

From this distance, in the weak light, the figure looked to be female, although that was basing his presumptions on the presence of the full-length dress and long wind tattered hair. She stood like a crumbling scarecrow, her head hung down as if shyly examining her shoes. It was hardly the time and the place to consider footwear. Completely silent, motionless; it was disturbing although he could not say exactly why. The hairs on the back of his neck crept up to stand on end.

It was a flash of an image out of the corner of his eye. So sudden it couldn't have been real, and yet the detail was so precise it seemed too much for a trick of the mind. The woman was right outside the car without having moved. She stood by the passenger side, staring in through the window with dead eyes. She was young, only in her twenties, yet she looked exhausted as if she had lived and struggled through a hundred years. Her long, light blonde hair hung tangled and limp, obliterating the outer edges and cutting through the lines of her face. Only her eyes seemed to be unobstructed, deeply focused, heavily outlined in black eyeliner and shadow to draw attention.

Aran slammed his foot on the brake and skidded into an emergency stop. Tyres burning against tarmac. Foolishness swelled up as he was flung forward on impact, his seat belt roughly catching him in a begrudging manner.

There was no one at the window.

The drive up north had taken more out of him than he realised. He twisted in his seat to look at the field. She wasn't there, probably never had been. He desperately needed to sleep. He put the car into first and drove onwards.

Framed by tubs of vivid red geraniums, Aran stepped out of the post office. He carried a local map, underneath which was a more embarrassing purchase, concealed like pornography, but far less stimulating: the locally printed book of ghost stories. Something for duller moments. The woman in the post office had given him a curious look as he had asked for a map, bringing the booklet from a shelf and passing it over to him. He looked like the type to be interested in that sort of thing, she had said.

Having unpacked the car that morning, he had driven back to the village. Whilst he was going to be here for some time, he might as well get acquainted with the area. His own road map was very sparing on the details of the area, so he'd bought an amateurish hand-drawn local walking map in the hope of getting a better appreciation of the area.

Wandering to the front of his car, he propped himself up against the bonnet and unfolded the map. The village was drawn out in detail on one side of the sheet, with every street name creeping down its respective road. Each item that was deemed to be remotely interesting was pointed out for those who cared to know. On the reverse there was a larger map covering the local area and it was this Aran was examining.

A small black outlined blob below the hills, child like on the paper, denoted the village. Several miles to the west of the village skulked Knight's home. It had been added on the map the way a hill or a turn off would be included to help people get a sense of direction, like an off hand land mark if you happened to find your way there. As a building in its own right, nothing was hinted at, the lack of words making it clear strangers were not welcome. Several hundred years old, the building could have had some limited tourist appeal in its own right, yet it was hidden like a guilty secret. It was as closed to the general public now, as it had been when it had first been erected. Still a very private home.

Aran's brow furrowed as a misplaced sound cut through the mix of birdsong and occasional hum of passing motor engines. As though someone was steadily shaking a large tub of beads, marching out a beat. The sound was growing closer. Lowering the map, he looked up, seeing no obvious source. In the periphery there was a woman approaching, but she was doing little else other than walking and carrying a can of drink that certainly would not be making the noise. Despite the heat, she was wearing a full-length jacket. The coat was a deep maroon and underneath the ankle-length violet skirt twisting around the movement of her steps. Her light blonde hair shimmered, ridiculously long, almost reaching her hips.

As she neared, he felt his throat tighten. He recognised her from last night in the fields. Last night at the car window. It was definitely the same woman, yet she was different today. Still pale, but somehow she looked healthier. He had convinced himself she had been a figment of his imagination. Her appearance mentally knocked him back.

Her eyes were heavily outlined in black eyeliner, smudged with shadow powder. Perhaps an attempt to be a goth but really just an over-indulgence in definition. The sound of shaking beads accompanied her steps, and now that she was close he could hear another sound, like loose coins in a hand. The breeze blew back her hair, earrings of thin metal disks the size of pennies hanging off silver circles were revealed. The jewellery jangled with the vibration of movement. Her eyes were downcast, either unaware or slightly embarrassed of the accompanying soundtrack.

She walked brusquely past and continued up the road through the village. Aran watched her progress until she disappeared from view. He had convinced himself that he had just imagined her, but she was here, living and very real. It was strange that she caused so much concern. He didn't know her. Why should he stop and wonder?

He jumped as the breeze snatched the map out of his relaxed fingers. Darting forward, he scooped up the paper from the pavement and turned it over to the street plan of the village. He ought to stop gazing after the local women like some impotent dirty old man and focus on why he was really here.

If he was going to write that biography, he would have to speak to the man and find out what had driven that unexpected retirement. Gaining access to Patrick Knight was to be a riddle. The first months following his retirement had released an inundation of journalists. Everyone had their inspired plot to tease out the real reason behind his departure from the political circle. No one got anywhere near close. The entire episode was still a completely closed mystery to the country.

The only way anyone was going to find out, was to get Knight to admit to whatever his secret was. Words from the man's mouth. It would have been easier communing with the dead.

All approaches to back researching had been covered and nothing had been dug up. Aran knew that he would need an angle, even if it were little more than a pretence, to get Knight interested in talking to him. Many tactics had been tested earlier. He had to find something that everyone else had neglected to consider. He needed something amazing, and perhaps a couple of years ago he would have managed it. His flair was petering out, and the best he had come up with was avoiding politics and feigning an interest in history. The Knight family residence had been built several hundred years ago. From just a brief glance at the amateurish map he had purchased, you could be surprised by the various historical remains packed into a seemingly empty area. It was enough to occupy even the most demanding tourist for a short visit. And yet this region wasn't a major tourist draw; the Lake District, Yorkshire Moors and Dales drawing off the bulk of the visitors to the north of England.

The Knight residence had never really been deemed worthy of feature on the popular tourist maps. Not even as a home of local political persona. It seemed illogical for a country where tourism was such a major industry. Under the pretence of writing an article about the hidden treasures of this area, he could have a plausible reason. Would it be enough? When the man had been an MP, he had made no secret of his interest in history. Clearly marking out his own interest in the preservation and appreciation of their country's past. He'd presented a dry documentary series on historical architecture. Something vague, Aran hadn't watched it and could barely recall the television reviews.

Thoughts trawling through his mind; but wandering aimlessly through the village whilst he plotted; he made no concrete signs of action. He paused, musing on whether he should drive in search of the nearest library or continue in his local exploration.

The road ahead was a no through lane, a single track of weather worn tarmac, pitted with potholes like a disease plaguing highways, warmed by the hot sun. At the corner, where the lane joined the main road, a metal sign was attached to a stone garden wall declaring to the uninitiated that this was Church Lane. Creepers held the metal plate in place against the wall; rich coloured flowers hung around the edge like a botanical border to barely legible words.

The church to go with the lane loomed up from behind a line of small cottages. The spire complete with the crucifix at the peak stood like a dark and foreboding shadow against the intense blue of the cloudless sky.

The lane took a sudden swing and came to a gritty end. It was rounded off with a turning point where someone had parked a green mini. By the car's tyres an unkempt verge of long grass sprung up, contrasting against the harsh grey of the gravel. There was a community centre that looked rather shabby and in need of funds. It reminded him of home. Not much to look at, but inside waited the real riches. He had grown up in various parts of Scotland. Out in the country visitors would refer to the more modern architecture as bleak and shabby. Those grey pebbledash buildings under equally grey clouds. There had been real heart and soul under those roofs, a feeling of safety and welcome, quite simply humanity.

Up at the end of the lane there was a split in the cottages with the track crossing over to the church. This way be God. So they said.

His eyes moved slowly back to the community centre. In the background was the sound of drained, faded out music. Someone was inside. He checked his watch, it was already half four. Perhaps the business of the community centre had already begun and an early evening class, possibly dance, was underway. The community centres from his childhood had rarely been quiet.

The front doors were a cluttered area of information slips fixed with tape to the inside of the glass door panel. There were pottery classes, a drama group, photography, ballet for girls, clubs for scouts and guides, conversational Spanish, beginners French, Tai Chi, belly-dancing, painting and a few different computer courses. Every group had its own amateur produced scrap of paper advertising times and course details. For such a small village, he was surprised that so much was on offer.

He scanned over the notices, looking for this day and time. There it was, in bold black handwriting in the far corner. Belly-dancing: Ludvine Moore.

The music abruptly stopped. A cloud of chatter and laughter followed. Aran pulled open the door and slipped into the cool, short corridor. He'd seen this current trend a lot: the fashion of taking up other cultures on a whim. Pretentious or just fascination with the outside world? Bored housewives shaking their arses and babbling about the goddess within. Christ, it had even made it out here.

The chatter ceased; a moment of silence before the music began. Pulsations of sound out of a doorway. Fast, rhythmic, filled with hard beats. It was a classy club track washed with heavy arabesque influence. Over the melody there was a warbling vocal singing in Arabic.

The corridor ended abruptly. A door propped invitingly open showed the way through to an enclosed grassy area. A small sun-kissed paradise perfect for going to sleep in. His eyes shifted back to the doorway where the music slid out into the corridor. It sounded like someone was shaking coins again.

A dance class was in progress. Eight women of varying ages and sizes, all facing the front of the room, stood with their right hands stretched out at Aran. The women were placed in three rows: a three, a four and finally a single woman up at the front who was presumably the teacher. The side wall was a line of full-length mirrors, sliced half way by the ballet bar. Movements and shaking loose flesh reflected back as they danced. A multitude of action and form, bursting with the women's exhaustion, the bright, vivid colours of their clothes. The dancers shifted position, facing him for a brief moment in the flow of a twirl, but it was only a skinny woman who actually noticed his presence. The twirl stopped and they stood with their backs to Aran. The skinny woman looked over her shoulder, flashing a smile as she flexed her exposed and over developed abdominal muscles.

They were involved in veil dancing; a lightweight, large transparent piece of cloth held between outstretched arms. Always up off the floor. Deceptively simple, but it was tiring holding your arms up for that long, as the back line of red faces would show. The cloth rippled like water. When perfected, the dance looked simple, requiring no concentration. When perfected. The women on the back row became tangled up in their veils. They tried to draw it over their heads and around their bodies in a graceful manner whilst attempting to keep their feet in the right places.

Every hip carried a vividly coloured sash. Multitudes of small coins or beads were sewn loosely into rows on the sash. With every slight movement, the coins would jingle against one another, and in turn the very movement of the coins only seemed to accentuate the original dance movement.

From that point the divisions became much more distinct. The majority of five, also the oldest present and the largest in the group were wearing T-shirts and either jeans or, with the exception of one, a long skirt. The other three, the dance tutor included, were in traditional dress: long skirts down to the ankles, short tops revealing stomachs that could use a little more sun. One girl had a vest top she had simply rolled up so that she could admire her abdomen in the mirror whenever they took a pause. The other two, including the skinny woman who had smiled at him were the most authentically dressed.

"Mrs. Davidson, push out with your stomach, not with your arse!" The teacher's voice suddenly jumped out over the music, breaking the almost hypnotic, exotic atmosphere with a rough jolt back to earth. Aran was intruding on a class. He stepped back into the shadows, out of sight. He would often forget himself. He was drawn by community and society; always observing even when work had finished. A photography obsession witnessed in cardboard boxes of shots. Not everyone appreciated his attention.

He retreated from the corridor and into the grassy clearing complete with picnic bench at the back of the building. There was a good view of the church tower from here. Viewing through the camera, he focused in. He carried a camera with him like an artificial limb, even when he wasn't working on an article. He always took his own photographs. The best photographs were always a split moment's chance.

The old picnic bench stood on a tilt as if an elephant had tried to sit on one end. The ageing wooden planks were covered in moss. Perching on the table top, careful not to slide down, Aran gazed up at the church spire. Apart from the music drifting out from the open windows, it was incredibly quiet here, truly peaceful. There was no rush, no panic, no desperate stare demanding to be the best, completely annihilating resources, neurotic desperation for everything now. There was something liberating about this kind of peace. This was like his childhood. Quite simply the lifestyle embedded in his nervous system. Some people were meant for city life, others were not. He probably should never have moved to London.

Noise echoed out from the corridor as the women began to depart. They trotted merrily to the front of the building, discussing who had the worst muscle pain, who was utterly confused and who had two left feet. Five women had departed. It was another minute before the thin women, the only one to have noticed him, slipped out. She paused, holding a small shoulder bag limply as she glanced around, expecting to see someone. The corridor was empty. She gave up, with a sweep of her skirts stalking out into the sun light.

Arabic music was playing, ambling at a relaxing pace, mainly instrumental with the occasional vocal sigh.

Aran strode back through to the dance room. He had not wished to be seen earlier, but now that the class had dispersed, he found himself pulled back through, wanting to be welcomed into this community spirit.

Only the teacher remained. Bare footed she moved across the polished wood floor, the light veil gracefully following to mark out the air currents. Her movements looked incredibly simple, no effort at all. This was the professional, the one who had been dancing religiously for years. She did not appear to be paying any attention to what she was doing. Yet as a dance form her steps and actions were very controlled. If the upper torso moved, the lower did not, and vise versa, to the point where it seemed as individual sections of her body, especially her hips, would move completely independently on their own accord. She paused, on an angle with one leg pointing forward, a wave moving down the flesh of her abdomen. She could not really be described as skinny, and had no obvious muscle formation unlike the pupil who had smiled at him. She just looked right, and with the shake of her hips, he was physically attracted. It had been a while since he had bothered to think of such things since the misery of his previous love affair.

She took a couple of steps to her right and tilted backwards as if to make a little swoon. Her long blonde hair hung back off her face and he recognised her as the girl who had walked past earlier, the same girl who had been in the field late at night. Now she was neither insane nor distant. Within his near vicinity yet still completely unaware of his existence.

The music changed beat and she started to move backwards. She abruptly stopped although the music continued, concentrating on a scrap of paper. The veil caught between two fingers, hung lazily, brushing against the floor. She was caught in a graceful pose, frozen part way through the dance. It made a good picture and the photographer in Aran could not resist.

She looked up sharply as the light from the flash burst out across the room. The image was broken. Irritation sank across her face as she stared at the stranger, realising what he had done. She was waiting for an explanation.

"I'm sorry, I couldn't resist," he said, lowering the camera. "I am getting a few local background shots, you know, to capture the culture."

"You're here to take pictures of local culture?" She did not sound as though she believed him. She had still not moved.

"Not exactly." Aran smiled lightly, feeling foolish at their misunderstanding. "I'm really here for the history." It was less of the truth than the first response.

"You're looking for history?" She raised her eyebrows, bemused as if he was not what she had been expecting.

"You don't have history here?"

She laughed out loud, for the first time visibly relaxing. "Yeah, there's history here. Just nothing worth getting excited over." She wandered across to the CD player, the beads on the sash jingling with every footstep. The music abruptly stopped.

"I think everything has at least one interesting story to tell," he idly commented, watching her. "Are there any archives in the village?"

"Archives?" She made it sound like a foreign concept.

"Libraries…"

She shook her head, a little grimly. "This place isn't big enough for anything these days," she said bitterly. "Lack of funds. Not worth the investment."

"So what do people do for fun here?"

She paused, smiling coyly as she regarded him. "Dance," she finally answered. "Take pottery lessons. Either that or drink themselves into oblivion. No one's ever been interested in history. Why would you be?"

"I'm a writer," he explained.

"A writer interested in culture and history?" She sounded as thought she was mocking him. "Do you work for the tourist board or something like that?"

The tourist board, now there was an idea. He watched her as she stood up, bag and CD player in hand. "Something like that."

"That must be a good job to have." No sarcasm. It sounded more like envy.

There was a tone in her voice that denoted disillusionment. He couldn't help it. She inspired empathy. He had to stop himself from touching her arm. He barely knew her. "Your life can't be all that dull. You've not exactly got an average job here."

The woman smiled grimly as she took a thick ring of keys out of her coat pocket. She turned and locked up the dance room. "Only one of many."

"You have another job?"

She stopped, pursing her lips and looking him straight in the eye. "You do ask a lot of questions. Have you ever thought of turning your writing talents to high-flying journalism?" She paused. "I'm actually the cleaner if you must know. Teaching dance does not pay the rent unfortunately."

"I'm surprised you get enough interest to hold any classes out in a place like this."

"So was I."

The conversation faltered, two strangers with no common goal in mind. Neither certain quite why the other was still in the corridor, still in this conversation.

"I'd better go," she started to excuse herself awkwardly, jangling the keys to remind him he had to leave. "Things to do, that can't wait for even the tourist board."

"You shouldn't take the power of the tourist board lightly," he joked.

She laughed. "Yeah. God forbid. I honestly can't figure out why someone would come here. Are you just passing through or are you staying in the area?"

"I'm here for a couple of weeks, but the sooner I can start my research, the better."

"Research," she muttered to herself incredulously. "There's nothing here worth researching. Nothing obvious anyway."

"So you mean to say there is something?"

"Could you do me a favour?" she interrupted, abruptly turning on him. "Could you destroy that photo for me?"

"That photo?"

"The picture that you took earlier," she reminded him. "Without permission I might add." She broke off, expecting him to agree to the offer, but instead he just stared at her. It made her feel uncomfortable. In truth, he was bewildered, caught up between two conflicting ideas: one that she was normal and one that she was insane. When she thought back over the impromptu conversation later in the evening, it had been distinct, him watching her as if she were an unidentified species.

"Anyway," she broke the silence awkwardly. Making inane conversation to calm the atmosphere, bring him out of the building. "Tell me, where are you staying? You haven't ended up at the pub, have you? Those two will talk you to death."

"I'm renting a cottage. It's a little basic." His mind had started to revolve backwards again. He was thinking of yesterday evening and growing confused. Today she was completely normal, or at least as normal as anyone could be dressed like that in such shabby surroundings. When he had first seen her in the field like a scarecrow, she had given the impression of being deranged. He was now sure that he had not imagined her but he must have because the facts were so contradictory. "It's just outside the village," he continued, noticing her curious stare, a reaction to his own expression. "A bit north, through two hills."

She nodded. "I know where you mean, one of Betty's old shacks. That will be basic." She paused again, tilting her head to consider him from a friendlier angle, her earrings making the same light metallic sound that was rapidly becoming familiar. Summing up potential. "Do you have a name?"

"Aran Sellere." He reached his hand across to her. "And you are Ludvine, I presume."

She smiled wryly. "It's pronounced Ludd-veen, but yes, that's me. Ludvine Moore."

Aran followed a skinny teenager into the community centre. The gangly being still hoping to grow into her identity had dyed green hair. She hadn't quite decided what she thought about anything. Almost walked into the door. In a trance, she followed the sound of music. Ludvine was here. He could tell from the music, that and the fact that her coat was hung up in the hallway.

He observed from the cool shadows of the corridor. The teenager was now lounging on the floor by the windows at the back of the room. A handful of other women, most in baggy T-shirts stood quietly talking. Up at the front, seemingly unaware was Ludvine. She was not quite so traditionally dressed, if traditional was the right word for a style partially inspired by old Hollywood films. Dressed in black like the cat burglar adapted to the hot summers. Only the sash interwoven strings of beads around her hips suggested anything more exotic. The beads moved from side to side as she rolled her feet from one side to the other as if pushed into motion by a light breeze.

Why he was here, he could not really say at present. It had nothing to do with getting an interview with Knight. No possible excuse for background research. He had just needed to come back. To see her again.

The dance class started up properly as the final pupils arrived. Aran felt uncomfortable, watching from the corridor. He retreated to the back of the building, setting himself at the picnic bench once again to wait for her to finish her classes.

To pass the time, he read the booklet of ghost stories he had been pressurised to buy in the post office. It started as casual flicking, arrogantly condescending the poor grammar and lack of articulation in the prose. He was soon engrossed in the stories.

As if plucked from an old Victorian penny dreadful, with gothic etched illustrations. It was a collection of anecdotes, of ghosts rattling their chains at midnight, local witches burned – hearsay with weak historical back up - reputed mad men and killers, short said the usual expected clichés. One paragraph caught his eye. Even Knight was part of local hearsay. Reading more thoroughly, he was introduced to the tale of a local farmer meeting the ghost of one of Patrick Knight's ancestors, fifteen years after the old man had passed away. One afternoon whilst the farmer was at the local pub. The farmer was a tenant on the Knights' land, and the old man had walked up to him and asked him when he was planning to sow a crop of potatoes. The fact that the farmer was at the pub most probably explained everything. It was bizarre that this drunkard's story had been preserved all this time, a hundred plus years after the event to be included in a Victorian book of ghost stories.

"Found anything useful?"

Aran involuntarily jumped. He had presumed himself alone, forgetting his immediate surroundings. His eyes moved up from the booklet, seeing a female hand, the skin rough and worn around the edges by physical labour, resting on top of the table. Moving steadily upwards he met Ludvine's gaze.

She had seen the title on the booklet, amusement caught in the corner of her mouth. He quickly stuffed the book into his back pocket.

"We always seem to meet under these circumstances. It's half eight. I need to lock up."

"Half eight?" Aran looked shocked. The last time he had checked his watch it had been nearing seven. He could not have possibly been reading this nonsense for an hour and a half.

He regarded her for a moment as he stood up. Real, sane. No ghosts. She was waiting for him to leave. You had to go through the community centre in order to get out of the garden. "I'd better head off. Been here too long now."

Ludvine nodded. They were now loitering by the back door, neither knowing if they should just walk away. Uncertain as to if it would be impolite to turn and leave. "Well, I have to lock up and set the alarm again."

"Right." He turned away from her, feeling a little foolish like a school boy with a bad crush. She didn't seem to be all that impressed with him.

He burst out of the community centre and into golden evening sunlight. The scent of warmed flowers thick in the air. He stopped by a dry stone garden wall, leaning against the rough, weather worn stones as he flicked through the scribbled notes he had made during the day. There was essentially nothing here he could use to convince Knight he was writing a book on architecture. The pretext for an interview to declare he was not a failure, that he was not a sorry excuse for a human being. He was hoping for a miracle, and either like a fool or a wise man he was stumbling blindly onwards without considering giving up. No matter how hopeless it seemed.

A line of crunching footsteps on the gravel made him look up. Ludvine came out from down the side of the building and began to walk towards him. She had changed, and gone were the dark clothes in favour of long dark jeans and a red vest top. Her hair was completely loose, flowing like silk down her back. She stared straight through him and walked by without uttering a word of pleasantry.

"You got locked up all right?" he asked, merely out of a need to say something to her rather than out of any concern for the community centre. She simply ignored him, not even worth listening to. Taken aback by her sudden dismissive behaviour, Aran stepped up from the wall as if to pursue her. "Ludvine?"

This time he had her attention, because she stopped. The automatic reaction upon hearing one's name. There was a moment of uncertainty before she twisted around on her heel to look back at him, to make sure it had been he who was talking to her. There was confusion on her face. "I'm sorry, do I know you?"

Aran's peered back at her in an equal amount of bewilderment. Perhaps she was working on the principle that she did not wish to be associated with him outside of the community centre, as if such a thing would damage her local reputation, but her confusion appeared to be sincere. Besides, there was no one else out on the lane to witness their conversation. "What are you talking about? It's Aran Sellere..." He did not know why he was introducing himself again to her, only a minute after they had last spoken.

"Right..." she spoke slowly, watching him guardedly as if expecting him to reveal himself as a lunatic. Yet she continued to approach, her curiosity caught and gradually being reeled in. "If we've met, I don't remember it, sorry."

"What, have you got a major short term memory problem?"

She laughed, taking his comment as a meaningless joke. "I sometimes wonder."

"Seriously," he started. Her behaviour could be marked down as amusing, but she was putting up the pretence a little too seriously. "You can't have forgotten. I was sat out the back, reading."

"Reading, right." She nodded as if to humour him. It was blatant from the look in her eyes that she did not understand.

"What is this? You have to be winding me up!" He relaxed as soon as the words were out of his mouth, guessing what she was doing. Having seen him engrossed in the cheap little ghost book perhaps she had thought it a fitting joke, or maybe she just enjoyed teasing people. The personality of a jester. Such a character trait would explain her odd little stunt the other night. "Is this 'mess around the outsider'? Make me think I'm going mad?"

"If you're going mad, you clearly don't need me to help you," she retorted in good nature. "I'm sorry that I don't know what you're talking about, Aran, wasn't it?"

Half-amused, partly frustrated, Aran couldn't let it drop. "You are messing with my head."

"Why would I want to do that? I have nothing against strangers. So what's the story? Did you just move in here?"

He studied her eyes. She was playing this pretence well. She was utterly convincing in her act of their never having met. "You don't have a twin…?" he started lamely.

"No!" She laughed at the thought. "Have you been drinking?" She boldly leant up to him, pretending to sniff his breath. "I can't smell anything. So why are you here? Please don't say you've already told me."

He did not know what to say now. He would just have to play along. "I'm a journalist. I'm writing a piece about the area. That's why I was here, researching."

"A journalist?" She appeared to be genuinely interested in him now, not just for the prank they suspected one another of. "Tourism?" she asked, presuming she was correct. "This place is the total opposite of publicised. I doubt you'll find anything of use in the village. There's never been much and a lot was destroyed a few years ago. But as for the area, well, there's a lot of interesting old things if that's what you're looking for. There's a lot of hidden history."

History could be a way in to Patrick Knight. The man who had moved back to his family home, a family home that was historic, intricate, laced with the memories of generations. "A lot of history? Like what?"

She stuffed her hands into her jeans pockets and shrugged absently. "Oh, there's the old church here of course, then the mansion… there's a Celtic cross, a stone circle, a barrow…" She broke off looking up at him. "But as I said, these things aren't exactly publicised. I'm not sure why. I know a while ago the Knight family stopped a lot of tourist ventures, but we're talking a good few decades."

"Can you show me where they are?" he asked, flicking through his note pad to the folded map.

"Well, sure, when I have the time, but…" she broke off as he produced the map. "Oh, you mean mark them off on the map."

"Yes. What did you think I meant?" He met her stare as he passed her the map. "Oh, right," he realised. "But if you want to show me yourself where they are, that would be great. Local knowledge is always the best."

He wondered why he was playing to the misunderstood presumption. If Ludvine was just teasing him then it was nothing to worry about. Yet he was not sure it was all that simple. She was taking this joke a bit too seriously. The mannerisms of her behaviour were so convincing it was possible she believed they had never met before. She looked innocent, but coupled with his first sighting of her out in the darkened farming land; it was always possible that she was mentally unstable. He started to doubt her again. It was hard, considering that pale porcelain face with delicate features, but anything was possible. It would be wisest to disassociate with a mad woman before getting too involved. Get out before you woke up one night to find her creeping up the bed with a knife in her teeth, enraged by irrational jealously and determined to hack you to pieces. That was logic. But he could not stop himself.

She tilted her head as she considered him, perhaps thinking similar things. Personal safety was a big issue these days. There was a smile on her face. "You are odd, but all right. Where are you staying?"

He knew that he should not answer but he did. "I'm renting a cottage to the north of the village. It's a bit run down, well, still being renovated…"

She nodded. "I know what you mean. One of Betty's old shacks. Well, I'll come over sometime in the early afternoon tomorrow and give you a tour… if that's suitable of course."

"No problem at all." Aran smiled back, wondering how much he was going to come to regret this.

The infamous cottage was as near to what he could call home, as his present situation would allow. It was a rustic building; in estate agent speak having character; situated down a narrow, rough farm track riddled with potholes like a virulent case of acne. The access route cut between two grazing meadows speckled with buttercups. The cottage was hidden from the passing main road by a slight rise. Further back a line of the forest's bravest trees stood beside a grass clearing substituting for a proper garden.

The single lane track petered out into an uncertain spray of gravel beside the cottage. Here it was, an old farm building that had been left to neglect for decades. The roof had been made watertight that spring and all the windows had fresh panes of glass. Electricity had been connected too although it seemed unnecessary considering the noticeable lack of built-in electrical items, including light fittings. Electricity was one of the few modern comforts he needed, if only to power the laptop computer and write his articles. He could compromise on everything else. The kitchen was virtually empty apart from a modest fridge, a portable two-ring hob top on the work top like an after thought and an old kettle. The fridge held little, the hob top took an hour to boil water and the kettle would click off randomly. Currently on the move, cutlery and crockery was something he still owned, packed away in a box in the bottom of his car. He did not need to rely on others too much. He could look after himself.

The living room was quite desolate. There was a high-backed, wooden framed armchair and a large empty crate posing as a coffee table. Nothing more. Aran sat on the floor beside the open patio door in a pool of hot light. A mug of cold tea stood waiting to be consumed, but forgotten. His attention was elsewhere, his fingers furiously typing into the laptop computer. Thoughts pouring out onto the white glaring screen, the floodgates inside his mind open.

Aran was in the habit of making regular detailed notes when working on an article. He tended to type out realms of information, most of which was never used. A recorded stream of consciousness, later to be picked over for scraps to feed the final work. A lot of what he typed was irrelevant. Over the years he had developed a comfortable working pattern, and his note taking had gradually transformed into a form of extensive journal writing. Every discovery and experience during the process of researching went down in these digital pages.

The current subject flashed at his face in black print. Ludvine. Puzzled views surrounding that name, falling into simulated words. Perhaps when his thoughts on the matter appeared on screen, the answer would become obvious and he would understand her odd behaviour.

Something tapped against the open glass door. Aran glanced up, half distracted from his writing.

"I'm not interrupting, am I?" Ludvine was peering in through the doorway. He didn't know how long she had been there.

"No. Why are you here?"

She rolled her eyes in exasperation. "You're not going to start on with that game of silly beggars again, are you?"

"So you know who I am?"

"Of course I do, Aran. My memory's not that bad." She gritted her teeth, keeping her patience. "I thought you wanted to see the local hidden sites, for this article of yours." She paused, peering at his computer as if to try and read what he had written upside down. "Although I do wonder if you're telling me the truth," she continued, as if thinking out loud. "I mean, a tourism article about this place. Tourists aren't interested in this area. Who's going to pay you for such an article? Of course, there are other points of interest. I don't suppose you'd be especially surprised if I told you that the ex MP Patrick Knight just happens to live here now?"

Aran smiled wryly, amused by her observancy. Territorially pulling down the laptop screen. "I couldn't possibly comment," he responded, sounding like those smug bankers and businessmen he had tried to interview in years past.

"Of course you can. I'm not writing an article about you. Tell me off the record."

"Why are you showing me around?"

His question knocked her off from the playful train of thought. She stepped back out into the sunshine, her hair gleaming under the intensity. "I'm bored, if you must know. Since I moved back here. Well, when you've been other places..." She shrugged, as if at a loss for words. "What can I say, your insanity intrigued me."

That was rich coming from her, but he made no comment. "Well, perhaps tourism is just a cover, but you know as well as I do that no one has been able to speak to Knight since he retired."

"So you're looking for an angle to get to him?" she guessed. "And then he will just break down and confess to you why he quit politics."

"Maybe he would, maybe he wouldn't. Maybe that's not what I'm going after."

Ludvine pursed her lips. She would get the answer eventually. She watched him closely as he picked up his camera and stepped out of the doorway. She was convinced he was investigating rather than suggesting holidays to the uninspired. When Knight had first retired, the village had been overrun by journalists, each with a more cunning ploy to get Knight to talk to them. All kinds of methods for sneaking onto the property. Of course, every attempt failed. Knight wasn't exactly stupid, and he was very determined not to talk. She did not really know Aran, but she doubted he would succeed where the rest of the country faltered and given up.

"So what's the first stop on our tour?"

"I thought we'd start with the stone circle. I haven't been there for ages and it's too far to walk so I need a lift."

"You haven't got your own car?" Aran questioned rhetorically, realising for the first time that she must have walked here. He was already aware that she knew the surrounding countryside very well, having seen her out in the fields, but he had just presumed that she would have driven out here. His car stood alone on the thin patch of gravel.

"I can't afford such things at the moment. Besides, I like to walk around in the countryside. Just not round there."

"Not round where?"

She shrugged and avoided his gaze. "Up near the circle. Come on, you drive, I'll give the directions."

Ludvine proved to be a forgetful navigator, frequently remembering to tell him to turn off when they were already upon or just passing the junction. Three times Aran had been forced to stop and reverse. It was a blessing that the traffic in this area was very sparse. It was a driving paradise compared to that which he had grown accustomed to in Greater London.

The road they eventually made their way to was single track and began in a good state of repair. But smooth tarmac quickly degenerated to rough gravel and finally to earthen ruts. As they rattled up the road, the vibrations of the vehicle jolting, Aran wondered what this must be doing to the suspension. For the most part it did not really matter, it was an old car and the journey up this road was far more worth the effort than refusing due to an over indulgence in a piece of machinery.

The road died in an unkempt clearing of grassy tussocks. Old gnarled trees watched from the edges. Perhaps it had once been a car park, but these days it did not look like much more that a patch of empty land, the trees scraped away from the centre. They left the car parked near a thick bramble bush, and clambered over a style in the wooden fence. On the other side was a steep hill washed with vivid green turf.

"I suppose you're going to tell me that the view's great up here." Aran commented lightly as he followed Ludvine up the hill. Considering the gradient he felt as though he was obliged to make a comment on the haul up to the top but in reality the exertion took little out of him. It was steep, but it was thankfully not too far.

"Hmm, what?" Ludvine muttered without looking back. "Oh, the view, right. I suppose it will be good up here."

The stone circle was hardly Stone Henge, and as he stumbled to the peak of the hill and surveyed the ancient monument, it felt as though this was the feeble end of the Stone Age, the poor man's megalithic monument.

There were ten stones in total, the tallest at nine o'clock from the head of the remnant. The stone was not tall, barely reaching his waist. All the rocks were rough and uneven, merely plucked from the earth and dumped into the ground on the hill. The rough, light grey surface was blotched with lichens of different colours and formations, adding to the texture of the rock.

"So why don't you like to come up here; is it a local place for bloody sacrifice?"

"The emphasis being on bloody," Ludvine laughed. "Looking for a sensationalist scoop? I doubt you'll find it here." She wandered into the confines of the circle. "I don't often come here because I don't often come here. That and because it's near to the Knight estate." She turned and caught a look in his eye. "Don't get excited, he's not into any dodgy stuff. No midnight rituals up here. In fact, he lives like a hermit. Like his own private monastery. If it wasn't for that great big house he has, you could easily forget that he exists."

"Have you ever been there?"

"To the mansion?"

He nodded.

She wouldn't look him in the eye. "I cleaned for him…"

"Of course," Aran realised, scolding himself mentally that he had missed on such an obvious choice. Cleaning would not bring in much money and she would have to take as many little cleaning jobs in the area as she could. It was so obvious that Knight would need someone to go in and deal with that great house. "So you'll know the house really well?"

Ludvine shook her head. "I only worked there once." Her words haltered, awkwardly staring out in the middle distance. Not sure whether to explain or leave it there. She was painfully conscious of Aran staring at her, almost willing the details from her lips. So what happened? "I had enough to do anyway, and… I don't know," she shrugged non-commitaly. "He can be a bit intense. Hypnotic."

She looked defensive. It was a bad subject. He was honoured, he guessed, to have got this much information from her on the matter. She was closing up now, perhaps closing too far. He didn't want to push the Knight aspect too much at this early stage. "What's the history behind this place?" he asked, deliberately changing the subject.

"There isn't really one," Ludvine responded. "It's just an old forgotten stone circle. No one really knows why they were built, and I don't suppose anyone ever will. It's been here four thousand years now."

He circled the prehistoric site from the outside, steady steps as if pacing out the circumference. The largest stone stood across the ring in opposition to him. As he crouched down to get a low-level photograph he noticed without comment the speed with which Ludvine stepped out of the circle as if scared of having her picture taken. He snapped off a few shots, standing up and moving around the circle to get pictures from different angles. It was of no real importance to his article, but for personal interest more than anything that he took the photographs.

Ludvine was watching him. "Are you a journalist or a photographer?"

He smiled. "A bit of both."

Lowering the camera, he straightened. He was now standing a few meters away from the largest stone. He looked over to Ludvine. She had moved back into the circle and was, perhaps disrespectfully, leaning against the tallest rock and gazing across into the distance. Her stare was intense, exaggerated by the heavy eye makeup; a signature feature like a birthmark. He wondered what she would look like without. Her long hair was drifting on the breeze, soft strands brushing over her face and cutting the image into blocks; her eyes, her nose, her partly opened mouth.

"It's stupid, the little things you miss when you're away for a while."

He did not know what she was talking about. "Have you been somewhere?"

"Yes, well, not really recently. I was over in Denmark for almost two years, working," she explained, tearing her focus from the scenery and meeting his eye. "I missed little things from home, missed them so badly. I was just looking at the lake, thinking how homesick I got for it." She laughed at the thought as if trying to hide the emotion. "And now that I'm back I just take it for granted again."

"It's human nature to take things for granted." He joined her by the head stone of the circle. "You can certainly see a long way from here."

"Yeah. Do you see the large building way out there?" She reached out with her arm as if she were about to pluck it from the backdrop of distance and pass it to him. "That's Knight's mansion. Although it doesn't look so big from this distance. Further back from that you can see the lake. The barrow I mentioned is on the other far side of that." She paused thoughtfully. "I don't think you can see anything else of major interest from here. Well, the village is back over there," she added as an afterthought, lazily waving her arm out in that direction.

Aran moved out of the circle to view the village. It looked like part of a toy set upon green felt, the church spire reaching up to the overhanging curtains of blue. He took a picture for the sake a taking a picture.

Ludvine stuffed her hands in her pockets and started to walk back to the track down to the car park. "You should just call Knight and get an appointment if you can. I don't know whether sight seeing will help you at all. The only advice I can give you is be as uninterested in him, and as interested in his house as you can."

Aran loitered by the circle. Perhaps she was right. A false sense of security of the highest degree might work with Knight. An interest in the house could not help but bring him into contact with a man who lived, according to local gossip, like a hermit. He followed Ludvine's tracks down the slope.

Cramped in the village's red public telephone box, Aran phoned Knight. He couldn't get any reception on his mobile. He'd spent an evening posturing in different rooms of the cottage, wandering around the garden and slowing walking down the track to the road. No bars appeared on screen.

Knight's telephone number was predictably ex directory. It didn't matter. Aran had ways of getting the information he needed. Contacts in the right places could get you anything you wanted.

The telephone rang five times before the dull thud of the receiver being picked up by unseen hands. There was a further pause as if this was going to be a bizarre kind of reverse crank call, then a male voice that could be no other than Knight spoke. "Yes?"

"Hello, my name is Alan Baxingdale. Might I speak to Patrick Knight?"

Lies before they even got to the set-up; but Aran didn't want to risk anything, including Knight recognising his name from some obscure article, back in the days when he was a journalistic heavy weight. He had wondered whether he ought to desperately dive straight in with the explanations, but had decided to remain casual. Calmly presuming that the man who had answered the phone was not Knight seemed to be the best introduction.

The voice on the other end of the line sounded slightly suspicious. "Speaking."

"Oh, I see." Aran was convincing in sounding genuinely surprised. "I am currently working on a book…"

"A book?" Knight interrupted sharply. "You're a writer? How did you get this number?" His infuriated questions tore up the cable. It was the start of a flood of demands that came relentlessly. "I will tell you the same thing as I have told all the other two bit journalists and mediocre writers who have come bothering me. I have nothing to talk about and you will not have my life story."

"But I'm not interested in your life."

There was a sharp intake of breath in the Knight mansion, as if this was a new insult. Knight had been about to hang up, but hearing this made him pause. He was knocked from certainty by this unexpected statement. The journalists had been so persistent; perhaps he had grown complacent and expectant of the unwanted attention.

"What?"

"I'm currently working on a book about the architectural history of this area. I was hoping to include a section on the Knight estate. I can do my research at libraries and the local records offices of course, but what I am really wanting to do right now is get some pictures, actually see the property in the flesh so to speak."

Silence responded. Perhaps Knight really was mulling the possibility. It had been months since the last of the reporters had pestered and plotted after interviews. The media world had given up, presuming the most credible possibility was that there was no gossip to be had. A few days of silence and you could soon forget anything had ever happened. "I can have your assurance that my name will be left out?"

Aran could not suppress the grin. Underneath his sane voice claimed he was striving for the impossible and making a fool of himself. That could all still come, but perhaps this daring project would be completed. Old colleagues and trusted friends said it was doomed to a non-start. They had given him understanding stares, mentioning that the past few months had been a terrible strain. Perhaps he ought to take a break from conspiracies and journalism and focus on himself. He would prove them wrong.

"Naturally," he assured Knight. "My interest is for the building, the history. I am not here to write a tabloid melodrama. Although your family name will have to be mentioned in reference to the estate of course."

"Of course," Knight agreed. "Just as long as no reference to the current owner, myself is made. Well, when did you want to come and view the property? I will have to be present."

Aran was stunned that it had come this easily. Knight must have taken him at his word. "Well, I'm working in the area for the coming weeks, so really whatever time is suitable for you. I can work my researching and other visits around it."

Knight cleared his throat down the telephone as he thought. "Well, best to do it as soon as possible," he muttered as if considering a personal agenda. "How about one o'clock?"

"Today?"

"Yes."

"That would be perfect."

"Very well then." Knight concluded the negotiations. "I presume you know where the estate is. I have good security here, so it's best if I meet you down at the main gates at one o'clock sharp."

"I won't be late."

"Good bye."

Knight hung up and Aran was alone without connection. He was an odd specimen for viewing, crumpled up in the old-fashioned telephone box. Still stunned that Knight had agreed to this meeting. Perhaps the man was so vain about his family home that he was temporarily blinded to the possibilities. It was very sloppy really, to take Aran at his word.

Replacing the telephone, Aran slipped out of the box and into the clear air. Only three hours before he would finally meet the legendary Patrick Knight.

Knight waited at the entrance gates. Neatly sliding into the role of lord of the manor since stepping down from political life; dressed in his green outdoor waistcoat, corduroy trousers, cravat and sturdy boots. Yet it was still the same Patrick Knight who had been frequently photographed for the more upscale newspapers of good quality, the same man who had achieved a rare thing in politics: a respect and a trust from virtually the entire country. A contradiction in terms. An honest politician seemingly. Something had changed since the glory days. It was not big, in fact it was barely noticeable, yet the man seemed to be withdrawn and closed off. He had taken his fill of the world during his career and he wanted no more. He wore a controlled expression, still suspicious of Aran, or Alan as they had been introduced, but pride over his ancestral home had overrided his sensibilities.

Knight strode over to the car as Aran pushed the driver's door open. "Alan Baxingdale?"

Aran responded naturally to the pseudonym. "It's very good of you to be so accommodating, Mr. Knight, I wasn't expecting to get an appointment so quickly."

"Well, I feel as though I ought to do my bit to promote architectural history. I do feel this area has been a bit neglected in the past, although I must admit my family had a little to do with that. They were not keen on attracting hoards of bypassers and tourists."

"You have a different opinion?"

"Not exactly. I would prefer to keep the skyline clear of rambling groups and crowds of tourist cameras. However, I am working on the presumption that your work will have a different kind of readership."

"Naturally," Aran lied. "I'm aiming for detail and accuracy. This will be a little bit more than a vague tourist pamphlet." His eyes drifted back up to the closed gates, moving past those sharp dark vertical slices of metal to the view beyond. The gravel road wound up a slight rise of neatly trimmed grass before reaching the Knight family home.

Knight smiled dryly at Aran's last comment, completely unaware of what was really happening. Aran was not exactly what he had been expecting for an architectural historian. He looked as though he would have been more suited to scribbling about mountain climbing and out door survival manuals, a quiet man out in the wilderness. Happy with nothing but his own thoughts for company. Perhaps he was a renegade mature student or something of that fashion.

"Well, if you wouldn't mind driving me up to the house, the tour can begin." Knight twisted slightly, taking something from his pocket and pointing it at the gates. There was a groan touched with electric strain as the two sections of the entrance began to swing open, allowing seldom seen access up to the estate.

With Knight in the passenger seat, Aran drove to the mansion. He parked just to the side of the main entrance, a dominating towering pair of dark wooden doors that peered down their noses at his scruffy car. The hand brake groaned petulantly as he pulled it up, reluctantly agreeing that the car might as well wait here whilst he took the tour.

Knight was soon out of the vehicle and stood admiringly in front of the family home as if it was the first time he had ever seen it. Aran was a little slower, releasing the safety belt before twisting around to get his camera off the back seat. Giving the driver's door a sharp but soundless kick - if not locked the latch was weakening and thus the door easily opened - Aran walked over to Knight.

"Would it be all right if I record the conversation?" Aran asked, holding a bulky and purposefully old looking tape recorder, to add to the image of someone naively trustworthy, someone who could not possibly be a 'journalist'. Even if Knight refused, he already had a small tape recorder concealed and running. This awkward machine was technically unnecessary, but it would save him from having to make a lot of short hand notes to keep up the pretence of being fascinated by architecture. "I didn't want to have to spend all the time making notes and not being able to appreciate the building. I'd rather look, listen, get a few pictures along the way."

"Oh, of course," Knight responded off handedly. A couple of months ago no journalist had managed to get anything more than 'no comment' from the man, regardless of the ingenious and cunning tactics employed. This laid back, unconcerned manner was near disconcerting. Perhaps Knight had simply grown tired of the defensive routine. He supposed anything was possible.

The Knight family home was a wide building when viewed from the front. Two storeys of light grey rock. Large, empty looking windows with the hint of heavy drapes behind stared down onto the neat, controlled spread of gravel in front. It was a blatant product of its time, caught up with a surge of interest in ancient Greek and Roman constructions that had captured European architecture a couple of hundred years ago. The main doors were decked over by a shallow portico, carved Corinthian columns stretching up to hold the top of the porch. On the top of the building there was a large stone carving. The carving was faint now from the effect of the northern winds, but on a whole it could be seen with the right lighting. It was a symbolic design, a kind of medieval schematic. When Aran asked about it, Knight had brushed the issue aside, muttering something about the stone mason of the time. If Aran really had been writing about the architecture, he would have pursued the matter further, but as the architectural history was in truth quite irrelevant he did not openly question Knight's evasive attitude.

Knight was surprisingly open with information about the building and spoke extensively. It was a large property, but from the length of time it took Knight to lead him around the perimeter, Aran felt as though they had covered the territory of a village at the very least. Knight was incredibly knowledgeable, even by the standards of any rich middle aged man coming from a landed family. He knew the reason behind every brick, every stone, every timber and every pane of glass that was visible. He was filled with architectural history, side notes on the building and planning, and anecdotal tales of the times when the mansion had been erected and extra features added over the generations. A vain monument to the Knight family, to their abilities, their success and their mind. Aran felt obliged to take rolls of film, now having documented every square inch of the building. Pictures too detailed to ever use for anything but the book he had no intention of writing. Wishing he'd brought the digital camera instead. He'd thought that arriving with one of his older cameras would make him look more plausible somehow.

There had been no clear opportunities to lead the conversation in any direction away from the house, no where close to Knight himself. As the informal tour began to reach its conclusion, they returned to their starting point at the front of the building. Aran did not want to give Knight the chance to swiftly shake his hand, say the tour had been nice and he would look forward to the book with that look in his eye of 'get off my property, heathen'. Aran said something about the gardens which they had seen from the rear of the house, and how he would like to get a couple of pictures before he left. Thinking now at this point of failure he should just blurt out his real questions, hope that the man's sudden fury would cause a lapse in all this secrecy.

Knight had not seemed to mind until they had reached the sun drenched sprawling patio at the back of the house, becoming guardedly restless as if he had just thought of something. Aran started to make vague appreciative comments about the lay out of the garden, or at least what could be seen, in order to draw out the time whilst he desperately tried to think of another way to get Knight to talk. There was something about the elder man's demeanour that made him want to be clever in getting the information.

"Well, the garden has changed dramatically over the years, unrecognisable now from the first years of the house. You really want to focus on the house, there's more than enough there."

"Oh yes, I agree. But the gardens have to be taken into consideration, after all, they do set off the house." Aran stepped up to a stone wall, like a miniature colonnade, that ran against the edge of the patio.

Holding the camera up to his eye, he peered through the viewfinder to the spread of the garden. His gazed moved from the aggravating exact lines of the flower beds to the rows of heavy fir trees, rose bushes caught up in clouds of insects, the small fountain at the head of the pathway. His eyes widened slightly as a figure appeared in the far distance from behind a long line of trees. Knight was supposed to be a hermit living in luxury. He quickly snapped a picture, lowering the camera and hoping Knight had not noticed the third person.

From the months of surveillance by journalists, a few facts had been gleaned. Knight lived completely alone. He employed no staff, not even a gardener surprisingly, and kept himself virtually locked away on the grounds. That there was another person on the property was unexpected. Naturally, it could have been a recently hired gardener or maybe a newly acquired cook returning from the herb garden. But there was something about the figure's countenance that was worrying.

He had not caught more than a second, and hoped that enlargements of the photo would clarify the scene. The figure had been a girl or a woman, ages always being hard to place. Late teens, early twenties in any case. Knight did not have children. What would a teenage girl be doing wandering about on private property such as this? Those questions aside, the most unnerving fact was that it had been blatantly clear that the girl was heavily pregnant.

Knight spotted the girl in the distance a few moments after Aran. Aran could sense the sharp turn in the air, the sudden tension. Knight wanted him to leave. The first mistake. Knight had perhaps neglected to consider all of the details when agreeing to this visit. Yet Aran had made no comment and appeared more interested in a statue close by. Knight decided that he had not seen the girl. "I actually have the original architectural designs for the house," he said, smoothly getting Aran to turn his back on the garden.

"Really?" Aran raised his eyebrows in interest. On the outside he was like a millpond. He honestly had not seen anything, because such a sighting would have raised some reaction in any genuine architectural historian. Knight presumed that if he had been a journalist, depending on his standing and ability, he would have taken one of two courses. He would have either started off into the garden on a pretence to explore or he would have shouted and waved at the girl, asked Knight who she was. Only a man who had not seen anything would behave as Aran was now doing. That was Knight's second mistake, relying on logical human behaviour and not realising that Aran now had photographic proof in his possession.

Knight eagerly led Aran into the house through one of the open French windows at the back. They entered a cool, shadowed private library, decorated in shades of deep moss green. The room was submerged in the sensation of thought. Shelves stretching from the floor to ceiling filled with rows of archaic books, leather bound and supposedly rife with ancient wisdom. Knight walked over to a large study table in the centre that gave the interior the sense of a real university library from an era now lost. In the centre of the table there was an old-fashioned desk lamp, as if study here went long into the night.

"This is a water-colour of the property by my great, great grandfather," Knight spoke, his back to Aran as he unhooked a painting from one of the few areas of wall that was not smothered by books. "He was a great painter. An artistic streak does run in the family. As I said, it was my ancestor who designed the house." He turned and carried the painting across to the table for Aran to view. "You can see some of the old garden design in the periphery of this picture. Now, as to where those old architectural plans are…" He drifted off, his eyes piercing through shelves and cupboards as if searching for the old documents by some kind of penetrating means. "I have so many drawings and designs here it is sometimes a little hard to keep track of them, I do…"

He was interrupted by the sharp tone of the telephone from a room somewhere on ground level. Knight's eyes widened. "Excuse me, I have to take that," he said, abruptly hurrying out of the room. He closed the door into the corridor primly behind him, to make it clear that Aran was not to go wandering whilst he was unsupervised on Knight's property.

Aran was not sure if this old library was the best room to furtively search for condemning evidence. He moved back to the window, but as expected, the girl had disappeared, as if a ghost. He returned to the exact, detailed, yet lacking in spirit watercolour. He picked it up, a cursory glance. Knight did not come from a line of great painters.

The painting had covered over a clutter of old books. One was a little larger than the others. There was no writing on the cover; it looked like an old ledger or journal judging by the size of the volume and the scuffed corners of the hard backed cover.

He opened it at a random page. It looked antique, handwritten in a malnourished style that was cramped and nearing microscopic. On the facing page he had chosen, there was also a black and white etching of a human figure, a man, kneeling down with his hands spread out. He had a cruel face, yet he did not appear to be anyone in particular, merely part of a diagram or a piece of instruction. Aran was intrigued, leaning forward to try and make out the script. "Transference…" he uncertainly read out loud a word.

A door slammed. Aran jumped automatically, closing the book and virtually flinging the watercolour down as if trying to put out a fire. When Knight returned to the library, Aran was innocently examining the painting.

"I am afraid something has come up." Knight spoke as he closed the door, approaching the table. "I am going to be rather busy from now on; our meeting will have to be cut short."

"Oh, that's no problem." Aran stood up. "You've been more than helpful as it is." He would have cursed his ill fortune that he had not got a word from Knight he could have used in an article. He would have revealed his identity, demanded the truth. But the unexpected appearance of the girl held his tongue. A lead to build on. He needed to be able to get back in.

Knight nodded, his face still, unmoving. "I'll show you back to your car." He gestured to the open door. They were to walk back around the exterior. He was not going to see where Knight lived.

Knight stood stiffly as Aran left his camera in the back of the car before getting into the driver's seat. "I can't remember where the architectural plans are at the moment. If I get a chance, and I find them, I will give you a call."

Aran nodded. "Once again, thanks for the help."

As he started to drive down towards the gates, he realised that Knight did not have any means of contacting him. Knight would be fully aware of that fact; he was not the kind of man who was ever forgetful or absent minded. It was a subtle hint that nothing more would come of this. A swinging contradiction, for Knight had invited him to view the house the same day as he had called. Why had he changed tact? The telephone call? Perhaps, but Aran couldn't know who it had been. For now, the best point to continue from was the girl.

He would have to develop his photographs. The supposed bathroom in the cottage, which literally contained a bath and little else, had a small window that could be easily covered over. The room could serve as a darkroom.

The car slowed as it approached the gate. Knight must have had controls up at the house, because the gates were slowly starting to open. Idly, he glanced across to a small gathering of trees, and was shocked to see the girl stood in the undergrowth, pale and tired, with a look that suggested her mind had been displaced a long time ago. What the hell was going on here? She stared at him, and began to shake her head. Don't do it. Don't do what? He could not stop and ask, as it would only alert Knight to the fact that he knew. Yet he could not just drive away.

He rolled his eyes at her as if to try and say, come here. No response. Why did he not shout? Knight would not hear from here. He rolled down the window. "Get in!" he called over to her.

The pregnant girl continued to shake her head. She crept forward to the edge of the trees. "Who are you?"

He was taken aback that she was the one with the questions. "Just a writer," he answered. "Who are you? I didn't know Knight had a daughter."

She looked as though she was going to cry. "He doesn't."

Not yet anyway. Was this why he'd abruptly quit his career. "What's your name?"

"My name?" she repeated the question as if confused. As if she hadn't been asked in a long time. "Rachel. Rachel Applegate."

Why did that sound familiar?

"You want to get away?" he guessed correctly. "Get in."

Her eyes filled with tears and she shook her head, backing to the trees. "I have no choice," she whispered in reply before she turned and disappeared into the undergrowth.

Aran had been developing his photographs for as long as he could remember. It had taken sometime to perfect the technique. Now that development was instinctual, he would never hand over the films to anyone else for processing, even if it meant creating a growing backlog. He couldn't trust anyone else with the task.

With the more personal, artistic shots, he would pour over the negatives, testing different strengths of developing fluid, and allowing different times to vary the mood of the picture produced. It was a period of reflection, looking back and reconsidering the moment. He could loose himself to the world, stop and really think. Haunting silence as the images, shapes and shadows appeared from the white paper, the liquid rolling like the slosh of a wave.

Today he did not have the patience to divulge into experimentation. He just wanted to get to the pictures. The question of that girl, odd and ghost-like in her wandering had been tugging on his mind. Her name; there was something about her name that meant something to him. Somewhere there was laughter, because a part of him realised that he should know already. There was something unsettlingly familiar about it all.

Normally, he would have been straight on the Internet, but he couldn't get any reception on his mobile to connect on his laptop, and didn't know where the nearest public Internet site would be. But he did know he had a photograph in his camera and he had to get at it.

In the back of his car, cramped up in amongst all of his personal effects he had all the items necessary for a rudimentary developing lab. Taking a broken board of plywood that he had found serving no obvious purpose propped up near the outhouse, he had covered over the solitary bathroom window. He changed the light bulb. He closed the door and began to unpack the equipment; pouring out liquids into trays out across the floor; tying lines of washing wire across the bathtub.

The hours wandered. Aran had no comprehension of their passing and demise. The heat gently dissolved from the sun and the light outside began to fade with the onslaught of dusk. Inside, caught up within the red glow of the bulb, Aran was tangled in this devilish twilight.

Finally he reached the picture of the stranger. He made a large print of the entire photograph, and some close ups of the figure in the garden using the original negative.

He snatched the pictures from the clothes line. Switching off the light, he hurried out of the bathroom, surprised to discover it quite dark out on the landing. Time seemed to have passed more quickly than he had sensed.

Tramping down the staircase, he flicked on the light to the spartan living room, and set himself beside the fort of cardboard boxes. He laid the photographs out on the floor. The girl's sallow face stared back, empty blank eyes. What was a pregnant young woman doing on Knight's estate? A girl who admitted she wasn't his daughter. It seemed secondary in importance compared to the fact that Aran was sure he had seen her somewhere before.

Sometimes these things happen. Amazing coincidences that confound the possibility it could be simple chance. There had to be a greater force at work. Something had to be behind the occurrence, because lucky chances like that simply didn't happen. He had merely glanced at the box beside him; containing research from a previous article. Idle fingers unconsciously taking a file. Flicking through. Starting to remember.

The picture in the file he knew he was searching for was far more cheerful. The girl was smiling, genuinely happy for the school photograph. Hair pulled back in a high ponytail. Sixteen years old. They had taken it from the picture frame, and tear stained, begged the public for help in finding their daughter. A good girl. A talented girl with so much going for her. They'd had news space for a couple of weeks, then the world got on with its life.

That had been a year ago. Aran picked up his own photograph and compared the two. A thinner face but a much more rounded body. A lot could happen in a year. It was definitely Rachel Applegate. One of two teenagers from Southport who had just disappeared, cliché style without a trace, one weekday early evening.

"Oh Christ," Aran groaned, lowering his head to his hands. Everyone had their theories about why Patrick Knight had left the political circuit so abruptly, but no one had thought it could be as bad as this. A great public image shattered.

Rachel Applegate and Tanya Cole had disappeared together. They would be seventeen now, still marked down as minors by the law. It had been almost a year. Now Rachel had reappeared, like a mindless creature. Incubating. A whole year cut away from everything. What kind of frightening misery had she endured? She may have lost her mind. It was something she would never completely recover from.

What ought he do? He had come here to recover and to write the biography that would define his career. He had really succeeded. But he had been hoping for political intrigue and conspiracy and instead he was digging up something sick and twisted. This was the breaking story of the decade. Of course, presumption could be its own enemy, and just because he had seen the girl on Knight's property didn't necessarily mean that the ex politician had a child-molesting fragment to his persona, but real life tended to follow the most obvious route. It was too much for a coincidence. Aran would have every national paper fighting it out to get the right to print. He would be a national hero. There was more here than just a story. It was not something he could wait with. An innocent girl was involved, an innocent who had already lost a year of her life. Now that the discovery had been made, the police needed to get in and rescue her. But he could not help the selfish thread in him: he wanted to wait, wanted to shock the country with the sudden and unexpected truth. He felt ashamed for even considering sitting on this, waiting until he had got the story printed before going to the police. The girl's welfare had to be first. Besides which, he would always be the reporter that had uncovered this dreadful kidnapping result.

He glanced at his watch. It was late now, and he felt drained by the day's revelations. He did not know where the local police station was. He told himself he was too giddy on the realisation. He needed some time himself to accept the fact that he was back on top and in the game. Feeble excuses lined up and told him he had to think of himself and his future. Prove them all that he had not lost it.

Tomorrow, he decided as he stood up glowing with new release. Tomorrow morning he would go to the police and report the whereabouts of Rachel Applegate.

Aran did not sleep well. Barely managing to loose consciousness, his mind ran over Knight. What he knew. What he could guess. What might have been happening up in that mansion all these months.

He had to cling to some decency of a citizen. The police needed to know. Early that morning he was parking his car in front of the post office. He intended to go directly to the police station, just as soon as he knew where it was. Probably the police station lay somewhere in the nearest town, a reasonable drive away. Cutbacks, don't you know. He felt increasingly restless. He shouldn't have left it as long as he had. A few hours would make little difference in the long stretch of life. Looking back it would seem like a mere second. Now it felt like decades.

Aran turned, joining the gaze of the rural post office to survey the village green. The summer relaxed against the early morning, the heat still cut out of the sunlight. Only a comfortable sensation and a rush of vivid colours. People were heading to work, considering the tasks of the day. School children enjoyed long summer holidays, only just reaching the bored and restless stage, never realising that they would come to long for these days in the future when reality would relentlessly bite and gnaw. Hindsight was not a gift when it was needed, and for now the children were just rising from their beds, rubbing eyes and wondering what mischief could be conducted today.

A man in the far distance of greenery taking his dog for a morning walk. A group of sparrows twittered mindlessly as they hopped in the grass around the base of a large horse chestnut tree. Occasionally one of them would flap its wings and spring into the air as if having something important to say. Closer up there was a line of park benches decorating the edge of the green. The wooden seats were painted in bright green; the paint peeling off in flakes. All but one of the benches was vacant. The solitary occupant, female, blonde hair bent forward in concentration, her back to Aran.

He recognised Ludvine immediately and crossed over the road to speak to her. Feeling as though a few minutes in her company would calm him, give him the strength to get this over with, bring what he had seen to the authorities' attention before getting on to the papers.

On approach, he could see that she was reading an opened letter. It looked like a formal letter, from the crisp white A4 paper and lines of black typing, illegible from the distance. She heard his footsteps, and defensively folded the letter before even bothering to raise her eyes to see who was entering her personal space. She gave him a weak smile and nod as a greeting.

"How are you?"

She shrugged, crumpling the letter and torn envelope in her fist as if her actions could provide a better explanation than any words could offer. "All right, considering," she added in a non-committal way, not really answering the question. She twisted towards him as he joined her on the park bench, propping the side of her head up on the fisted hand that still held the beaten remains of her letter. "Did you get your interview with Knight?"

Knight. It reminded him of why he was supposed to be here. Still the shock of what could be easily inferred, clashing against Knight's public image. No one really knew the public figures, not who they were as people. "I went to see him yesterday. Told him I was writing a book on architectural history."

"And you got in?" Ludvine raised her eyebrows. "Well, this is why you're the professional."

Aran wondered what exactly she meant by that. There was a touch of bitterness in her voice, although not directed at him personally. He knew better than to ask.

"Did you manage to tease the truth out of him, then?"

"No," Aran responded, staring intently at her as she gazed out across the village green. He ought not to tell her anymore, either in order to protect his story or because the police would not want the general public to know. What was really happening on the estate still wasn't confirmed, although everyone would draw the obvious conclusions. He needed to confide in her. As if to get a second opinion. A validation that he was not going mad. "I did see someone there though. I don't think Knight realised."

"I thought he was living like a hermit up there."

"So does everyone else," Aran said, passing her the photograph of Rachel Applegate walking out from behind the line of trees. "But I saw her there."

"A pregnant girl," Ludvine commented lightly as she took the photograph from him, holding it at one corner as if not wanting to leave fingerprints upon the surface. "He doesn't have any kids of his own, that much I know. I wonder who she is."

Of course she would not immediately think of the missing teenager story. It was almost a year old, and runaway teens seemed to be such a common place mini drama these days. "Her name is Rachel Applegate," he informed her. "She went missing in Southport about a year ago; her and a friend just disappeared."

Ludvine looked horrified. "And she's just suddenly turned up? At Knight's?"

"Not officially. He doesn't know I saw her there."

"But..." she drifted off, looking back at the picture. "She's pregnant," she pointed out the obvious. "Please tell me you're not hanging onto this for maximum glory."

"I'm actually heading to the nearest police station, well, just as soon as I find out where it is."

Ludvine grimaced. "You've got a long drive ahead of you. They closed all the little local stations around here a long time ago. There is a police constable living in the village, Will Staple, you should go and see him now. You really want to get this reported as soon as possible."

"Where does he live?"

She twisted in her seat, pointing with an outstretched arm to a little side road going up past a cottage three houses down from the post office. "See that lane there? You head down there till you get to a little stone cottage with a great monkey puzzle in the front lawn. It's on the right, and you most definitely can not miss it. Will's house is the next one on from that one, a non descript house." She broke out into a wide smile. "No point trying to describe it because there's nothing to say about it, and I don't know what the number is."

"Right, thanks." Aran stood up from the bench.

"If the crime is solved, I suppose you'll be heading off again soon," Ludvine idly commented, leaning back against the bench.

It was a point he had not really considered. What would he do now? He had only been here a few days, but he had felt as though he was almost settling in, growing attached to the familiarity, the run down yet homely nature of the little cottage he was renting. "Not yet," he answered, making a decision. "There's the aftermath to cover, plenty to keep me busy. Besides, I've got the cottage booked for a few months."

She smiled. "Well, if you want to do a tourist piece, and need to see the sights, just let me know."

He felt a sensation catch in his chest. Hope maybe? "I will. Look, I'd better head off, I don't want to miss this constable."

"No, you don't. I'll see you around."

Following Ludvine's directions, the police constable's residence was easily located. She had been wise in directing him to the neighbour's house, with the prominent tree like an overgrown sentry in the front garden. In contrast, Staple's home had no distinguishing feature, a dull little building that would be hard to remember. The estate agent's ultimate nightmare.

Waiting on the front door step, having knocked firmly on the door, he could hear the sound of a radio from within, and was thankful that the local copper was in. Going through the local channels first would probably be the best way to handle this case. It would be the quickest way of getting in there and setting the girl free.

The door opened and a tall, well built man who probably could have made a good career in professional rugby on his physique alone, peered out at Aran. One eyebrow raised and a piece of toast grasped aggressively between his teeth. He had an expression on his face that suggested people without a good reason for interrupting his rushed breakfast would have all hell to pay.

"Constable Staple?"

The man nodded gruffly, plucking the toast from his mouth. "And what do you want?"

"I need to talk to you."

"You need to talk?" he sounded utterly disinterested. "Well, they have telephone lines for that sort of thing. Now, if you don't mind getting out of my way, I have to get to work."

"This is work," Aran cut the dismissal, not allowing Staple's sheer size and off hand manner to intimidate. "I don't know whether you remember the case of two missing teenagers from over Southport way." He produced the newspaper clipping that he had kept for his file. He did not expect the constable to immediately recall all the facts, after all, as of yet it was not even a local case. "I found one of them, only a few miles from here."

Staple took the old crinkled newspaper clipping, holding it in one bear paw as he silently flicked his eyes over the main details of the story. He shifted his gaze back to Aran, and there was still something there that did not trust him, that thought this odd stranger was going to be a problem. "Got something you want to confess, mate? Normal people don't usually keep…"

"Oh, quit with the intimidation," Aran interrupted, irritated by Staple's attitude. "I came here to report that I've found her. She's up at the Knight estate. And she's heavily pregnant."

Staple's face darkened. "That's some accusation to be throwing around," he muttered, stepping forward to glance down the lane. They were the only people there. "You'd better come in. Nothing spreads quicker round here than gossip. Village full of old birds with nothing better to do." He pushed his door further open and let Aran enter. He checked the surrounding area once more for enemy agents, before slipping back into base camp.

The interior of the police constable's home was equally non-descript and impersonal as the exterior. As if to suggest that the occupant was so lacking in character that the ability to leave a mark in a home was lacking in him. When he left, a sign of existence never remained. Yet when Staple was in the room, he was dominating. This was just his bachelor home and he had never been one for home furnishings and decorations. He only had here what he needed to live, what he required for the present moment. Melissa would have been particularly attracted to this bulk of a man. The thought surprised Aran; the image of his ex lover suddenly lurching up. He could not recall having thought of her once since arriving. It was a shame she had to make an appearance now in any shape or form.

Staple shut the door and stalked into the living room. "This is one hell of a serious accusation you're making, and you know as well as I do how Knight is respected around here, well, in the country. That man's got a big reputation. You'd better have some proof."

"I do." Aran passed him the two photographs, the original picture of Rachel walking in the gardens and the close up he had made of her figure. "These were taken yesterday in the gardens behind Knight's home."

The constable's large fingers clamped around the photographs. He slowly looked back up at Aran. "I think you'd better tell me what's going on. Knight's turned to the quiet life. He's alone. No one goes up there, do you understand me? What were you up to yesterday?"

"Knight invited me."

Staple forgot himself for a moment and looked incredulously at Aran. He did not look like the kind of person that Patrick Knight associated with. Not that the retired Member of Parliament associated with anyone these days. "You'd better start from the beginning."

As if he was on trial, as if it was unimportant that a girl who had been missing for a year now had turned up on a solitary, middle aged man's property. "I went over to see the family home. Knight was giving me a tour around the architecture. I'd called up yesterday morning, telling him I was writing a book about the architectural history of this area and I wanted to include the Knight estate. I saw Rachel in the gardens whilst we were round the back of the house. Knight doesn't know that I saw her, let alone that I got this picture."

"Architectural history? You don't really look like the type."

"I'm not," Aran confessed casually. "I'm an investigative journalist. I really wanted to get to the bottom of his sudden retirement. I'm going to write a book."

Staple smiled coyly, as he finally understood what was happening. "The first journalist to get in. Something must be said for that. Although I don't suppose Knight told you anything."

"No, but I found out what I wanted to know."

Staple glanced back at the photographs and newspaper clipping still in his temporary possession, grasping what Aran meant. "Your editor know about this?"

Aran shook his head. "I'm freelance. I won't have any problem getting a paper to publish this though."

"I suppose not," Staple said thoughtfully, considering the photograph. "Although I am going to have to request that you hold off selling your story. We can't have Knight reading in the morning papers that this girl has been seen, before we have a chance to do anything, now can we? All right if I keep these photos? Have you got anymore?"

"No, I only managed to take the one picture."

"Right, well, I'm going to have to get on to my superiors straight away. Glad you did the right thing. There would have been other journalists who would have gone straight to print with this." He paused, watching Aran, almost as if it was a fault, to have scruples in this modern age. "I'm going to have to talk to you again of course. Where can I get a hold of you, where are you staying?"

"I'm renting a little farm cottage, it's north of the village…"

"Telephone number?"

Aran shook his head. "It's pretty basic." He didn't hand out his mobile number to members of the police force as a rule.

"Christ, you must be stuck in one of Betty's half-finished shacks," Staple realised, a look of exasperation as if Betty had caused him problems in the past. "Well, I know the one you mean, so I'll be able to get you there…" He glanced back up at Aran as he finished scrawling something on the large block of paper beside the telephone. "You're not planning on leaving the area yet, are you?"

"Not yet."

"Of course not. You've got yourself a big story. Well, when or if you decide to move on, let me know beforehand, all right?"

"Of course."

Staple tore the sheet of paper from the top, folded it up and stuffed into his back trouser pocket. "I'll have to show you out, I have things to do and people to see." He strode towards the front door again, carrying the photographs and almost pushing Aran out of the building.

"Let me know as well what's going on," Aran told him as he locked up. "Like you said, I could have sold my story first."

"Yeah, yeah, yeah, your journalistic rights will not be impeded. I'll let you have the exclusive," Staple commented sarcastically as he stalked to his car. He sounded as though he was accustomed to dealing with journalists. Considering the attention Knight had come under when he had first retired and retreated back to his family home, it was an easy presumption to make. Staple had probably been called over several times to deal with the journalists, paparazzi and photographers that had swarmed at the closed gates like a contagious disease.

Aran watched him drive away. That had not gone exactly as he had been expecting, although he was not sure what it had been during their discussion that had unsettled him.

Restless and unsettled, Aran had hurried back into the village. He hoped that Ludvine would still be there. He wanted to spend the day, or at least part of it, in her company. But she had already departed from the bench, and not knowing where she lived he had no way of contacting her. He might have asked in the post office, but they would probably refuse to hand out the information. This being a small village, it was prone to gossip; she would soon learn that he had been asking about her, a fact in itself that might put her off. They were barely acquainted in the honest truth, and he did not want to appear over keen and desperate. Odd to think that he already thought of her in such terms.

Caught up in limbo there seemed to be little else to do other than wait. He was not sure what to do whilst Staple went to his superiors. He drove back to the cottage, taking up his regular haunt in the pool of sunshine beside the open French windows. His legs in faded jeans were stretched out across the thresh hold, laptop computer set in front of him as he furiously typed, pouring out thoughts like sand, frightened it might run out. Editing and pasting from the sheer bulk of writing, he completed the article that he would send in. A prologue to the book he would work on here.

The article was a great piece of writing, and with the photo that Staple had borrowed, Aran's work would be front page news, good enough for every paper in the country. This was his moment, his great story. He supposed there would be newspaper groups with offers of jobs afterwards, but would he take any of them? It did not seem to be an immediate issue. He did not even have a permanent base. He did not know where he was going to go next. Exciting and terrifying in equal measures.

Late in the afternoon he dozed off. He woke up in the dusky evening, his head resting against the door frame, the cool evening air rushing in through the gap. Glancing blearily over the lap top screen that broke into blaring life again in response to the jolt as he shifted his legs. He switched off the machine and put it to the side. He stood up and stretched, drawing his body out of sleep.

Trudging up the staircase, he entered the bathroom at the top of the landing. The normal light bulb had been replaced, and when it was switched on it sent a sickly, hollow glare out across the grubby room. Lines of photographs, long dry, hung wavering in the trapped air. There were countless shots of brickwork, windows and architecture that peered meaninglessly back at him. Aran sifted his way through the images back to the first pictures he had taken. He returned to the stone circle, finding a shot with Ludvine captured within the frames. She was unaware, dark eyelids cast downwards in silent thought.

Aran lowered the picture as he caught sight of the dance photograph he had taken the first time they had properly met, the image she had protested about. Taken on a whim, something for fun, for background, nothing serious. It had come out really well. The focus, the lightening and even the composition fell perfectly. He sat down on the edge of the bath to consider the work. Ludvine caught forever in her youth as an arabesque dancer. She looked stunning. Utterly graceful. His eyes ran down the curved side of her body, wondering what she was doing now.

His lips tightened to irritation as he noticed a fault in the photograph. He must have let the colours run or maybe the negative was faulty. Perhaps dust on the lens. At the right hand side of the picture the colours and lines of the background were waved, as if under the effect of shimmering heat. On closer examination, the run did not go down the full length of the picture, in fact it was contained to a very restricted line, as if it was some kind of odd shadow.

Cursing under his breath at the mere suggestion there might be something wrong with the lens in his camera, a lens he did not really have the finances for replacing at present, he looked to other photos for confirmation. He still had the stone circle with Ludvine shot in his hand, and was irritated to see that the same odd wave of darkened colours, like a floating shadow hanging ominously in the bright summer air. Twisting around, he pulled a photograph at random from the line, this one a shot of Knight's home, expecting to see the same fault, but this picture was clear.

It suggested that the lens was fully functional, but Aran needed to know what was at fault. Perhaps it had been that particular roll of film. Pulling down the remaining stone circle shots, he flicked through them, almost wanting the fault to appear again, but it was absent from all. It could not be the film, but it logically it could not be the camera either. Surely it would have shown up on several images. He turned back to the two pictures. The dance shot of Ludvine was in portrait form; the longer sides of the picture vertical. The shadow was off to her right. In the image of the stone circle, it was also to the right of Ludvine. But this picture was taken in landscape format. The fault had nothing to do with any of the technical aspects of photography. It had shifted with her. It was something that had been present at the moment he had pressed shutter release.

He inwardly jumped at the sound of movement downstairs. Tossing the pictures into the dry bath tub, he hurried to the bathroom door, surprised to discover just how tense he was. He had never thought that a fault on a photograph could have unsettled him, but he was not so sure that it was a simple developing problem.

There were footsteps in the living room.

"Who's there?" he demanded, thundering down the staircase to the empty living room.

Shock slapped his face as he discovered Ludvine stood in the middle of the unlit room. Her hair was loose, hanging in tatters and cutting up the clarity of her face. She was wearing a long ill fitting white dress, the same garment from that first night when he had seen her in the field. Having spent more time in her company, Aran had come to the conclusion that he had imagined that bizarre first episode, but now finding her in his house, wearing that dress, she really must have been there that evening. With sinking realisation he also saw that there must be something wrong with her.

Ludvine had a glazed look on her face, as if she was under the influence of something and no longer really understood what was happening. She looked gaunt, positively ill and frighteningly pale, so much so to be virtually transparent. She was solid however, breathing and barely living, a strange fragile creature that had just wandered in through the open French windows.

"Ludvine," he started gently, a touch of sadness in his voice. It was such a tragedy that someone as fascinating, as alluring as she was suffering from what he could only presume was a mental disorder. It was the only way to explain her odd behaviour. "What's going on?"

She ignored his question and began to walk towards the staircase. As she passed him he could see her face close up: the hollowness of her cheeks, the empty sag under the eyes, the glare of illness in her skin. It was such a dramatic change from what he had seen that very morning. It was difficult to comprehend.

Ludvine proceeded up the staircase in a steady slow pace, as if carefully testing each step under foot before trusting it to carry her weight. Aran doubted there would be much weight to hold, judging from what little body appeared against the ripple of the dress fabric. Her emaciated look was over exaggerated by the bad choice of clothing, but he was surprised to think that he had never noticed her thinness before.

The girl stood at the sink in the bathroom, her arms hanging limply, hands dead weights, peering into the mirror at herself, not recognising the dull, tired face that disinterestedly glanced back in her direction. He stood behind her, gently grasping her bony shoulders, wishing there was something he could say to her. "Come on, let's go downstairs."

She ignored him, and did not move, barely even appearing to breathe.

It was as if all preceptory senses had closed down. Perhaps she was asleep. Maybe she was a sleepwalker. It would explain that awful dress, perhaps a bad choice in night wear, and also her slow, dream like behaviour. Aran had heard that it was not wise to try and wake sleepwalkers up, and let his hands slip down from her shoulders. He ought to make certain that she did not hurt herself. He hoped that she would lay down and go to sleep. Backing off, he reclaimed his seat on the edge of the bath and gazed sadly up at her. He wondered what was going through her mind right now. Were her dreams nightmares, terrifying barren lands with strange beasts in pursuit?

She unexpectedly blinked and started to come to life. Peering into the mirror with a new focus, she reached up to her face. Her lips parted to reveal her neat, straight teeth, a natural family perfection. She fixed her thumb and index finger around her second upper incisor on the right. Aran felt his stomach start to turn.

She started to move her hand back and forth in small jolts, all the time keeping her fingers firmly fixed on the tooth. The tooth in question soon joined in with the movement, at first only slightly but swiftly it loosened to a full swing. Redness welled up to line against the gums.

There was a sound of meat against bone as she pulled downwards, sickeningly drawing the tooth from her gum without even flinching. The tooth, with full root attached, clattered into the white enamel sink as she let go; casting it away as if removing loose hair from a hair brush.

Ludvine turned away from the sink and walked out of the bathroom. Aran staggered up, not quite able to believe what he had just witnessed. The evidence was there, the tooth lying near the plug hole, the red blood contrasting garishly against the grubby white of the sink.

"Ludvine!" he started, marching out of the bathroom and hurrying down the staircase to stop her from whatever it was that she was intending to do next. She needed help, defence against the illness that was eating her up from the inside. Yet she was gone. As he hurried out of the French windows and into the empty surrounding land, he felt the solitude sink back down around him and realised that he was alone.

The next day the story had not broken in the nationals. By now the police should have raided the estate, Rachel Applegate saved, yet the scandal was not in the public domain. Knight's bad habits were still his own personal secrets and not property of the nation.

There had been no raid. If there was one certainty the world could rely on, a stronger bond of consequence than night after day and eventual death, if the police had acted yesterday, the papers would have printed the story. The only thing to travel faster than bad news was gleeful gossip on the scandalous downfall of others. Staple should have given him the word to print. Why was he even waiting for permission from that troglodyte?

Nothing had happened. Even the atmosphere in the village was that of a lazy, uneventful summer morning. The bored housewives had little to talk about, as he overheard in the shop, they had been forced to resort to discussing old news, things that had happened, months, even years ago.

Camera slung over his shoulder, he roamed aimlessly without thought or direction. Worn out from the old rush. His better self would have already sent a copy to the editor. He did nothing. Just read the local rag. His focus was centred on the newspaper, scanning over the headlines, the national stories, the current issues of the day. Nothing much had changed since he had fled his old life.

Folding over the paper, having taken his immediate fill, he looked up, surprised to discover that he had wandered in the direction of the village church and was now close to the small, slightly scruffy community centre. The front door to the building was propped open with a brick to tempt fresh air in to clear out the stale atmosphere. He stood and watched as a woman carrying a green plastic bucket heavy with water staggered out. Emerging from the shadows to light. Ludvine, now in her working form: pale khaki shorts and a worn, misshapen T-shirt. Her hair swiftly bundled up onto the back of her head. She bent over an open grating to the side of the main entrance and poured the grimy water away. Letting a relieved sigh go as if she had just freed the village from the last of a devastating disease, she set the bucket near to the doorway before dropping exhaustedly onto a bench up against the wall.

She was leaning forward, her head in her hands when she heard the crunch of his footsteps and looked up, squinting against the sunlight to stare with disinterest. "Oh, it's you," she spoke off handedly. "Have you come back to continue your local history research?"

Aran could only presume she was being sarcastic considering that she knew why he really was here in the village. There was certainly something, an odd change in her attitude as if she was drying up towards him. Perhaps this was a part of her problem, some kind of personality fault, although he did not even want to try to diagnose her, knowing little of the psychiatric world. Still, he ought to say something; such problems could not be ignored. But how to broach the subject? Simply saying that he thought she was clinically mad would not have the intended effect.

"I was just taking a walk," he said, tilting his head as he considered her face. All her teeth were present this morning. "Is that a false tooth?"

"What? Where?" Ludvine looked fearfully around her, as if there was a false tooth furtively creeping up on her.

Her reaction was almost amusing considering they both must know what he meant. "I meant in your mouth," he spoke, tapping the corresponding tooth in his own set.

Her expression darkened, warily considering him, shrinking back against the wall. "No it is not," she muttered, offended. Quietly she wondered if there was something comestically wrong with her teeth. She had never had anything done to them as a child. Whilst all the other children trotted around with metal wire strapped into their mouths, strange sleeping gear to try and pull their bone formations into a more socially accepted shape, she and her father had been quite happy with her the way nature had intended. "I've only ever had the one filling, that's it. Although I don't know why I'm telling you."

"So you're telling me that you have no false teeth?" He would have reached in and gently pulled it out if he could have been sure she would not have bitten.

"Yes, that's exactly what I'm telling you," she retorted angrily. She had only come outside for a break from this dull job, and had not been expecting a tirade of insults and insinuations.

"And you didn't pull it out last night?"

"No!" she almost shouted at him. "Do you have some kind of mental problem?"

His unspoken questions thrown back at him only suggested her ignorance to her own insanity. Although was it not said that people who were mad generally were not aware of the fact? "Sorry if I'm disturbing you," he sighed, sitting down beside her and noticing her shuffle to the far end of the bench. "This all came out wrong. I'm just worried, that's all."

"Worried?" She raised her eyebrows. "You have a strange way of dealing with anxiety. Is this the way you always begin all conversations when you're under stress?"

Aran laughed at the thought. "No, really, I'm quite normal," he assured her. "It's just that I'm worried, worried about you," he started to creep up to the pressing issue more carefully this time. "After last night. I mean, you seemed so normal, up at the stone circle…"

"The stone circle?" Ludvine interrupted him in confusion. "What are you talking about?"

He did not seem to be expressing himself very well. "I just meant that when we were up at the stone circle, you seemed normal."

"Up at the stone circle?" she repeated. "I've never been up there with you."

"Yes you have!" he protested, shocked how she could be so serious when she was throwing such blatant lies around. "The other day. You were playing at tourist guide."

"I was not. I don't know what you think went on, but I have never taken you anywhere." She paused, her expression turning to suspicion. "This isn't some attempt at some really bad pick up line, is it?"

"No. I'm not winding you up." Perhaps he sounded a little too desperately serious, almost offended. As if to suggest that the thought of chatting up Ludvine completely repulsive. He could see that the same thought flashed through her mind. Another thought was in her face. Whatever he might say, she did seem to believe that they had never visited the local stone circle together. He did not know if there was anything he could say that would persuade her otherwise. "The thing is, I am worried about you. Can I ask if you've ever suffered from any mental problems before?"

"You may not. I don't know what you think you're doing, but the last thing I need right now is virtual strangers coming up and insulting me. If you're worried about mental problems, perhaps it's your own you ought to be concerned with." She stood up and marched away, departing from the community centre, her work and her responsibilities and heading in the direction of the church.

Aran was quite literally baffled. "Well, where are you going now?"

"To visit my father's grave," she shouted furiously over her shoulder just before she disappeared from sight. As if it ought to have been obvious to him.

Aran jumped up from the bench and hurried in pursuit, as if concerned that she was going to hurt herself. Maybe this was an unstable panic attack coming on.

The churchyard was a jumble of scattered headstones, yew trees and narrow gravel pathways, taking mourners, visitors and the occasional morbid soul through the confusing arrangement of local burials. The church was a dramatic piece of Norman architecture, heavy in gothic influence, rearing up amongst the chaos. A solid, grey stone building, designed to outlive humanity and a statement on the mortality of man. It was impressive, with its noble yet deferential arches, and wind-weary gargoyles, all built to honour a God that Aran had not believed existed for a long time.

The church spire was located at the far end. It looked as though it had been added to the building at a later date due to the more intricate masonry than the gothic period would have considered. Beyond the spire the graveyard suddenly mushroomed in extreme size. The burial tracts pushed outwards into the countryside, generations and centuries of locals buried, old skeletons and dust mingled with earth concealed beneath the well kept turf.

His footsteps decreased to a slow yet definite crunch against the gravel as he came to the head of the spire. He could not see Ludvine. He momentarily forgot his pursuit as he was distracted by a long fenced off area of graveyard that ran in a straight line, like a direct continuation of the base of the church spire. At high noon the segment would lie in the shadow of the spire. It must have been a family plot, sectioned off by green metal railings. The vertical shafts like ornate spears denoted in no uncertain terms that strangers were not welcome on this hallowed ground. The headstones contained within were lined one after the other in the surprisingly long enclosure, as if every corpse under the earth was lying feet to head, stretching away from the church.

Aran tugged his camera off his shoulder, and crouching down took a photo. He had never seen anything quite like it. A few years ago he had worked on a project of old churchyard photography. The result had been a book of pictures that had been bought by a few people, probably all who knew him and made the purchase out of curiosity, but beyond that the book was not much of a success. Bargain bookshops did what they could to shift some copies. He had felt it was some of his best work. Realms of atmospheric shots capturing the commonplace features of the well-established British graveyard. Perhaps it had been a morbid, macabre idea but that had not been the intention. It had supposed to be inspirational and artistic. Beautiful, ethereal images held within the carvings, architecture, the manner in which nature grew out of the monuments to the dead; the yew trees, the grass, early morning dew and blackbirds pulling worms, the moss and lichen forms slowly spreading over the older gravestones.

He wandered up to the side of the indulgent private plot and read the inscription on a randomly chosen head stone. Robert Knight. He ought to have realised. Patrick Knight's arrogance in his family history, the greatness of the Knights should have been a warning that there would be such an over indulgent feature at the graveyard. It was personal yet very hostile, making it clear that if you were not one of the family then you were most certainly not welcome. In a wry moment, he wondered which side the railing was supposed to be keeping out.

Steadily he walked backwards, down the length of the family plot. The original Knight who had purchased this piece of churchyard must have been sure of his family's future success and importance. Sheer arrogance and elitism even in death. Keep the supposed cream of the nation separated from the commoners. It seemed almost paradoxical that a man who came from such a background could have won the respect of the nation in a way that suggested he was the just friend of the poor man. Everything Aran had seen since coming to this little village suggested otherwise.

"You got caught by the family memorial. It does tend to grab your attention the first time."

Ludvine hovered at the end of the graves, the empty stretch afterwards that was presumably waiting for Patrick

Knight and the descendants he did not have. What they would do when the plot was full? Perhaps the first Knight had known in his great wisdom when the masterful line, like all good things would end.

"It's pathetic, this hereditary sense of self importance," she commented, scowling at the line of graves moving like a runway back up towards the church spire. She seemed to have calmed down, as if having forgotten about the previous questions into her mental health. She folded her arms, the movement pulling the creases of her T-shirt downwards.

"You don't like the Knights?"

She shrugged with a look that suggested it was really quite unimportant. Her eyes ran up the line of graves, like standing dominoes waiting to be pushed over. "One interesting thing I never thought of before," she spoke, almost as if she was thinking out loud.

"What's that?"

"There's no women buried here."

"What?" Aran's lopsided smile was uncertain. Surely the wives would have taken their place in the family burial, if only with a small inscription at the bottom of their husband's ornate gravestone.

"No women. You can go through and read all the headstones if you like. I don't know where the wives ended up when they passed on, but they obviously weren't important enough. Well, they were never real Knights, just married in."

"But what about the daughters? I suppose they must have been buried in the family plots where they married in... if the families they married into were a little more open minded."

Ludvine shook her head. "I remember Dad mentioning something about that. Local history. They never had any daughters in the Knight family, only ever one son at a time. They were always a strange bunch." She let her shoulders droop, relaxing as her tension dissolved. "Anyway, that's just hearsay and little else. Fodder for tourist gossip. I've got to get back to work. I've still got somewhere else to clean."

Giving a little sigh as if to say 'somebody please save me' whilst fully aware that no one would, she trudged past him and wandered back up towards the community centre.

Aran turned back to the Knight burial site. One day Patrick Knight would take his place in this long line. It was presumed that Patrick was the end, but Aran had seen evidence to suggest something to the contrary. Rachel Applegate was carrying someone's child, and Aran would put money on it being Knight's. The next in the succession. It was not a family to be proud of. Aran hoped the child would be a girl.

Aran was at the stone circle. Avoiding everything that he ought to be doing. First introduced through Ludvine, the two – man and stones – were alone together on the grassy hillside.

He attributed his lazy behaviour to wanting to keep an eye on the Knight property. From the vantage point he had a good view with a pair of binoculars. Nothing much happened during his surveillance of the property. He saw nothing of the girl, Rachel. Knight's small figure, unobservable from that distance with the naked eye, went out of the building at about two in the afternoon, wandered around the garden. He did a little weeding before retreating back into his family home via a side entrance. As a subject to spy on from a distance, Patrick Knight really was very dull.

The police did not arrive to investigate the allegation of a missing girl held prisoner at the estate. Aran wondered what the delay was whilst he flicked more thoroughly through the newspaper and ate his lunch – tasteless sandwiches from the local shop. Perhaps the authorities were being extremely cautious, even on stake out. Patrick Knight's high public profile and influence would make anyone consider a raid more seriously than they would have done so had the suspect been an unknown, socially irrelevant person. Double standards in policing. Not that the police or anyone else had exclusivity to those double standards. The man or woman in charge would set the credibility of their career on the attack - a career that would afterwards be stamped down into the mud by the heel of Knight's boot if the evidence did not hold.

The girl was enough. Aran had a photograph of Rachel in the gardens, or rather he had owned one, which was now in the possession of the police. He decided by early evening, having given up on his spying, he would go and speak to Constable Will Staple about the matter and ask what was being done. If the answer was not satisfactory, he could always threaten to go to the nationals that evening. After all, the article was already written.

Will Staple was not at home when Aran had called. Lethargic in the heat, he didn't want to begin a long drive looking for the nearest police station. A small voice reminded him there was a moral obligation, but he took little notice of it. That voice of sanity, conscience or whatever it claimed to represent had been fading for months. He would try again in a few hours.

Not wanting to go home to an empty cottage, he redirected himself to the local pub. He had felt the need of mindless company, to listen to unimportant chatter and discussion.

Bill and his wife, Adele provided the escapism, taking it in turns to talk to the newcomer when they were not serving other customers, obviously locals from the way they spoke to one another. Aran weakly hoped that Ludvine would put in an appearance that evening, but she never walked through the doors and he did not dare ask the patrons about the eccentric yet curiously beautiful creature living somewhere in the vicinity. Instead he allowed himself to be distracted by Bill's talk of a village fete planned for the following week: a tradition going as far back as local memory and hearsay. It sounded like the usual affair for a small settlement out in the countryside: a moment to gather and gossip, be entertained and enjoy the summer before autumn swept down and sank its claws into the earth.

Nearing midnight he left the pub and returned to Staple's home. The second visit was later than he had intended, beyond the socially accepted cut off point for dropping in on a stranger. Staple hadn't struck him as the type for early nights and lots of sleep. The house was submerged in darkness. Perhaps the man had been sleeping, but Aran tried the door regardless. It made no difference. No response.

When he returned to the village green, the atmosphere was unsettlingly still and silent, the small streets empty. He was alone. He still couldn't settle. Wide awake and reluctant to drive home, he took a midnight walk through the village, experiencing the old narrow streets and the well-preserved country cottages in the twilight hours.

Wandering aimlessly over the village green, he came to an area he had never really seen. It was tucked away at the far side from the main road, almost as if shy of attention. He sauntered down the lane, passing by houses and small cottages cluttered up together when building had less to do with planning and more to do with getting roofs over heads. It reminded him of the place where he had spent his early childhood.

The buildings pulled back, the road narrowed to a single track of pummelled stone and gravel. Aran realised he was coming to the village boundaries. It felt empty here; a patch of woodland to his left, the track winding out in front with no suggestion of where it went. There was one more cottage a little further out of the village, and beyond that there was nothing but the wilderness, what would be a spread of lush grassy meadow when the sun was shining.

The sound of footsteps from behind broke the tranquil state. Aran turned and was mildly surprised to find Will Staple only a few meters away. "I've been trying to find you this evening," Aran spoke to him, only thankful that he had finally found the constable and neglectful to consider the odd nature of their meeting. "I wanted to talk to you about the photograph I let you have."

"Well, that is a coincidence," Staple spoke, a sliver darkening in the tone of his voice. "I've been up to exactly the same thing, and finally I have found you."

"I wanted to ask what the police are doing," Aran continued as the constable began his approach. "I gave you that photograph yesterday morning, and nothing has happened. You people have a duty to get that girl out of there, regardless of Knight's status."

"You really don't know what you're talking about."

"All right, so I can't say I know the details, but I know I saw Rachel Applegate. The girl was pregnant. It doesn't leave a lot to the imagination. It's been a year since she disappeared. That girl will be traumatised for years, for life."

"No she won't."

Aran was knocked off guard by Staple's random contradiction. Words failed him for a moment. "What are you talking about?" he questioned as Staple stepped in front of him. "Of course she's traumatised. I saw Rachel Applegate, she was..."

"No you didn't."

The comments came out like those of a stubborn three-year-old, contrary and desperate to be awkward. Rudely interrupting the other speaker.

"I've come to pass on orders to you." Staple continued, slipping back into an adult pattern of speech. "And the fact is that that girl is not traumatised, because she has never been on the Knight estate, and it follows that you never saw Rachel..." He held up his hand as Aran started to protest. "We all know some roaming nut killed them months ago. It has nothing to do with Knight."

"What's going on? Are the police scared of Knight?"

"You will forget about that photograph," Staple continued undeterred.

As Staple spoke, reeling off commands, reality started to clarify. The police as a national unit had not had the choice to fear arresting Knight because they did not know about the photograph. Aran stared in disgust at Staple. "You haven't told anyone about what I told you."

"Don't be ridiculous, of course I have!" Staple scoffed. "I couldn't sit on a thing like that." He paused, leering in threateningly close to Aran. "And I can tell you that Knight was not pleased when he found out he'd been tricked; Alan

Baxingdale. He'd done pretty well up to now keeping the reporters off his back…"

"You went to Knight." After all these years in this work, he could still be surprised at his own naiveté. "I'm going to the police, I'm going to the press, I'm going to print. I'm not going to sit on this."

"You're not going to do anything, because nothing happened."

Aran refused to be threatened. He had been born stubborn. "I don't know what he's paying you, or what you're going to offer me, but I am not going to keep quiet."

"Oh, but you will," Staple set him straight. "And don't expect a cash sum. All you're being offered to keep quiet is your health."

"What?"

Staple's fist hit his jaw unexpectedly, before he could consider the implications. Set off balance Aran staggered back over the rough lane. For the first time he noticed just how deserted and quiet it was here. A place where there would be no witnesses, and Staple was approaching again, pushing him further away from the village. Aran straightened, prepared now for the attack. He was not aggressive by nature and tended to avoid fighting if he could. He rarely got into any trouble, but liked to think he could take care of himself when and if the need arose. Yet the sight of the tall, bulky figure of Staple approaching did not inspire confidence in him.

"Bloody reporters," Staple looked disgusted. "You'll forget your bloody little story and everything you saw."

The constable threw out a second punch at Aran, who nimbly dodged the strike this time. In defence he hit back, slamming into the side of the opponent's jaw with considerable force. Staple's face was flung to the side on impact, and the attack only angered him more. It was like fighting with an aggravated wasp. It would not stop.

Filled with rage, Staple was unstoppable, a beast that worked for the highest pay, who had no loyalty but to himself. Mercenary of the first order. His tightened fingers were like a rock, smashing into Aran's stomach. Aran crumpled up in response, the shot of pain reeling through his body, tearing the air from his lungs. He felt as though he was suffocating. Another hit came to his face and a sudden rush of warm blood came pouring from his nose, streaming over his mouth and dripping from his chin. Despite the agony, he had a moment to feel sorry for himself, to feel ashamed of the weak presentation of a man he was, being pummelled and beaten and not managing to continue with his poor self defence anymore. All thoughts were torn from his head as Staple knocked him to the ground. Lying on his side, Aran was kicked, hearing the anger scream above him, radiating down like heat.

"You'll forget everything you saw." Staple yelled furiously at his victim. "And if I hear anymore of this, you won't be walking away next time." He gritted his teeth as he inflicted another kick. "Scrap your bloody story and bugger off back to where ever it was you came from." Leaning over, his weary drool dripped down onto Aran's sweater.

One final kick, almost half hearted and lacking in the previous viciousness, struck against the side of Aran's face. He felt a taste of blood rush through his mouth on impact. Aran clenched his teeth together. He listened to the sound of Staple's retreating steps, finally opening his eyes again to see that he was completely alone, lying in the darkness, a pathetic and bloodied form. An idiot.

Rolling onto his back, he groaned in agony. Little more than a mass of pain, soaked in his own blood. Down on his right shin, where Staple had kicked, a throbbing ache pulsated violently up through the leg. He would have to walk on it because he had no desire to go to hospital. His abdomen moaned from the beating. His hands were raw. His nose was numb, and gingerly reaching up, it felt as though the bleeding had ceased almost as quickly as it had started. The area that was giving him the most concern at present was his jaw, which ached as if someone had savagely torn away the lower part of his face. Perhaps his jaw was broken. He opened and closed his mouth several times, and despite the pain, the action flowed easily. Perhaps it was only superficial damage, although under this degree of pain, it was hard to believe. Gingerly reaching into his mouth to inspect the damage, he instinctively went to the loose molar tooth. He gave it a gentle knock and the tooth moved fluidly in response. Jesus, Staple really must have had some force in that kick. The tooth came out, half the root, one of the prongs, attached.

 Aran stared miserably at his bloodied tooth, feeling the blood flow in his mouth. Filling up the fresh wound. Twisting, he spat onto the darkened ground, listening to the sound of blood and saliva slap against the stones. In anguish he threw the tooth away. In his torture, his fear, he did not really care what happened to that missing girl anymore.

 He considered his surroundings for the first time since the beating. Staple had forced him further down the lane that he had realised. He was now sat outside the far cottage, which had ignored his tormented plight completely. A small building, slightly squat as if it had shrunk in height with old age. There was a brass plague beside the door. Leaning forward, Aran squinted, trying to read it in the moonlight. 'The mathematician knows all'. Some eccentric putting up ridiculous plaques for the thrill of it. No comprehension of real life. He had taken his fill of this village and it had finally made him nauseous. He did not care anymore. He just wanted to go home, and the tragedy of the situation was that he did not have a home. This story had been a last attempt clutch at some dignity, some meaning with his life. His career suddenly looked the mess it was. The mist had cleared and he could view his life from an impartial stand off. He had no home, no town where he felt an affinity, and he was alone, sitting in a lane in the dark, bleeding and beaten.

Carefully pulling himself onto his feet, he apprehensively put his weight onto his right leg, half expecting his shin bone to snap under the pressure, but nothing happened. Staple had done him the courtesy of not breaking his leg at least.

Angry and full of self-pity, he hobbled back along the lane towards the village green. He would get in his car, drive home and sleep, hoping this had all been a bad dream.

Coming out onto the narrow road by the village green, he collided with a hurrying figure bursting from the shadows. The figure let out a yelp, staggering backwards. Aran looked away, ashamed of what he could only imagine his appearance to be. "Sorry about that," he muttered, hoping to be left alone.

"You scared the life out of me," Ludvine's voice responded. He heard the sound of her step as she moved closer. "Aran? What are you doing creeping about?" she questioned. There was a friendly smile on her face for recognition, but when he turned to face her, the expression transformed to horror as she saw the blood. "Jesus, what happened to you?"

"Kind of obvious, isn't it?" He had not meant to sound quite so sourly sarcastic, but it was said now. He smiled weakly, as if to make light of the pain he was in.

"This is about that missing girl you were telling me about, isn't it?" she guessed, stepping up to him and peering at the blood, trying to make out where the source was. There was genuine concern on her face. Her stare only seemed all the more intense from the heavy colouring that she always wore around her eyes.

"I think she will be remaining as missing."

"But, you..." she broke off, reminding herself that this was not the moment for a discussion on morals and ethics. There were more important things to attend to. "Are you really hurt? I think maybe you should see a doctor..."

"No need," he assured her with a casual wave of the hand, wishing now that she would go away. He could feel the blood in his mouth again, with a growing desire to spit it out. "Just a few bruises, it looks worse than it is. All I lost was a tooth."

"A tooth?" Her eyes widened. It was as if she had never heard of beatings, locked away in her own innocent fantasy world where bad things rarely happened, and when they did, they were conducted with some kind of natural justice. The good never died young. "Jesus, who did this to you? You should get that fixed, the tooth I mean," she continued, not giving him chance to reply.

"No need, I'm heading home."

"Really, you should." Ludvine responded stubbornly, grasping his arm. "If you lost a tooth you'll be bleeding, probably need a stitch. I know a dentist here; his wife goes to one of my classes. We can go see them now. He's got this surgery here…"

"Ludvine, it's nearly one in the morning!"

"So?" She looked blankly at him for a moment. "They're insomniacs, let's go."

It was futile to argue. Relenting, he followed her up the village green. Ludvine glanced across, watching how he tried to keep the weight off his right leg. "Hurt your leg as well?" she asked. "Really, you should tell the police. We could go to Will St…"

"Stop." He came to a halt in the street. "If I am going to let you help me, if we're going to this dentist, there's to be none of this talk, these questions. I'll tell you this if only to shut you up." He paused, twisting away to spit the blood out. "Sorry about that. Staple did this. I don't know what Knight is paying him, but he did this to keep me quiet."

"Oh Christ. I know Staple is a bit of an arsehole, but I never…" she broke off, looking nervously back at Aran. "And I sent you to him."

He managed a smile, despite everything. "This isn't your fault. Come on, let's go visit your insomniac dentist."

The village dentist, to whom Ludvine referred as Mildew the moment he opened the front door, was a balding, chubby man with round glasses and tired eyes. Despite her claim that he was an insomniac, it would seem that he had since found a cure, because he had answered the door in his pyjamas and dressing gown. Yawning as he regained consciousness. Sighing, as if this kind of behaviour was to be expected of Ludvine, he led them through to the small surgery where he worked. Bright lights blared in the sterile room. The basis of so many people's nightmares, the black chair of torture, was at the centre. Aran had never been keen on dental visitations but had already suffered a lot tonight and one piece more seemed like a trifle not worth being anxious over. Besides which, he wanted the gaping hole in his gums to stop bleeding.

Mildew soon had him on the chair, reclined back with the light over his face. Rubber gloves snapped against his skin, and he turned around, a dentistry mirror in one hand. "Well then, let's have a look shall we?" he muttered, peering into Aran's mouth, poking at the wound. Satisfied that he knew what needed to be done, he withdrew. "Can you wash your mouth out with this," he requested, passing over a plastic cup of pink liquid. "It gets hard to see with you bleeding. Most of the tooth has gone, do you still have it?"

He shook his head. "You couldn't have put it back, could you?"

"Probably not," Mildew sighed. "There's part of the root still in there, quite a big part of the root. I'll get that out, then we might as well just stitch up your gum and let it heal over. If you want to get a false tooth you can do that some other time. I won't be able to stay awake that long. It's up to you though, it's not necessary. If you can live with the gap…" The dentist broke off as he drew a stool across to sit on. "I just hope whatever you were fighting about was worth it. I'm not going to ask," he paused again, glancing across at Ludvine. "I hope this isn't your doing."

"I don't fight with people."

"You know what I mean." Mildew responded to her flippancy. "Now, Mr. Sellere, I'll tell you the truth. I'm tired, we're doing this quick. There'll be no anaesthetic, so be prepared."

Ludvine grimaced, suffering sympathy pains. "I might go wait somewhere else."

The door to the surgery opened and a weary woman with fading red hair peered in. Mildew's wife. "What is going on here?" she questioned, bewildered, looking from Ludvine to the strange man lying back in the chair.

"Mr. Sellere here has just lost a tooth. I'm just going to quickly stitch up the damage, dear." Mildew spoke.

"Oh dear, what an awful thing to happen," his wife sighed, not really listening to what he was saying. "You won't want to stay and watch, will you Ludvine?" She turned to the girl, already bored with the grim dentistry news. "Come into the kitchen and have a cup of tea with me, won't you, I'll never get back to sleep now."

Ludvine and Mildew's wife vanished from the scene, settled comfortably in the kitchen environment with cups of tea whilst Aran lay in the dentist's chair and suffered. It was a swift job, and thankfully Mildew managed to remove the remaining root in one piece. Mildew stitched up the gum and cleaned the damage. With one final cup of mouth wash, he sent them back out into the night.

Whether due to a feeling of guilt or a genuinely considerate nature, Ludvine had refused to leave Aran, and had even driven him home on the basis that someone who was limping and had just suffered dentistry without anaesthetic was in no state to drive. They had cut through the darkness, fleeing the village and its residents, and back to the refuge the little isolated cottage that Aran currently called home. Parking up outside the building with a jolt, Ludvine had energetically hopped out of the driver's seat and merrily flung the keys in Aran's direction as he slowly drew his aching body from the car. "God, that was good," she gasped. "I haven't driven in ages."

"And what are you going to do now?"

"I was going to walk back, but…" She checked her jacket pockets. "I must have left my torch over at Mildew's."

"You can't walk back in the darkness now."

"Well, technically I can and I have," she corrected him with a lack of seriousness. "But that's not the point. Is it all right if I stay here?"

"Of course." Aran spoke awkwardly as he unlocked the French windows. The cottage was lacking in an obvious front door, so this had become a temporary main entrance. His jaw was aching. The bone felt like rusted steel he could not move. Mildew had warned him he would be a bit tender there for the next couple of days. "It's the least I can do after all the help you gave me."

"No problem." Ludvine stepped into the living room as he flicked the light on, glancing at the stacks of cardboard boxes and plastic bags, the remnants of his life lined up, some unpacked, others stored away for later reference. On the move and looking for somewhere to stop, to belong. She recognised the state of being. She shut the French doors and pulled down the latch. "How are you feeling?"

"Not too great, but I can't expect much more right now." He was still waiting for the painkillers that Mildew had given him to take effect against this agony his nervous system was being dragged through. He hoped that the painkillers had not started to work yet, that this was not the best he was going to get tonight.

Dropping his keys down by the closed laptop, he shrugged off his jacket and draped it over the top of a taped up box that he thought contained books. As his eyes moved over to the kitchen, he realised someone had been in the cottage. He had left his developed negatives on the kitchen table in a white box. The box was now lying on its side, the negatives spilled out like intestines. He did not need to check to know that the negative of Rachel Applegate had gone. Staple must have come here, broken in and collected up all the evidence. Perhaps that was what Staple had been doing whilst he had been sat in the pub listening to Bill chatter about village fetes. "You can take the bed, there's only…"

"Save the chivalry," she interrupted. "You look like you're about to crumple. You want to go sleep this off. I don't think I'll go to sleep anyway. I'll just roll up in a blanket and wait for first light, then I'll let myself out and walk home." She paused, glancing around in search of something to sit on or roll up in. "Do you have a blanket?"

"Sure." Flicking back the lid of a box, he pulled out a tartan blanket, the kind of thing that people generally took with them when they went on picnics in the countryside. Those strange people who were happy. Aran had it to lie on when he was 'researching' for a story, or more simply put, spying on people and waiting for individuals to turn up. Photographs for incriminating evidence. "I'm going to head to bed now."

"Night." Her lips wore a strange sad smile as she accepted the blanket. She turned and shook it out before slinging it around her shoulders.

Aran loitered, wanting to say something but unable to think of any words. His mind was exhausted, his body in pain. Joints were starting to freeze up. He would try to sleep if he could. Leaving her sat in his usual place by the French windows, he climbed the stairs and entered the only bedroom that could be described as furnished. Flicking on the light, he glanced around the bleak surroundings. White walls running down to a scruffy wooden floor. The only item in the room was the large bed, little more than a mattress on a platform. A duvet lay crumpled on one side, like the sleeping lover that did not exist. Turning the light off again, he kicked off his boots, and dropped into bed fully clothed.

Head resting on the pillow, he closed his eyes and tried to decide which was strongest: the throbbing pain in his mouth, or the one in his leg. There was a lighter ache in his side where Staple had punched him that came in at an unimportant third place. The painkillers would do no more. He drew the duvet across his body. There was nothing more to do than wait until he was too mentally exhausted to allow the pain to keep him awake. The more he focused on falling asleep, the more awake and conscious of the pain he became.

He couldn't stop the thoughts roaming, as much as he wanted it to just all stop. The memory of the thrashing he had got that evening. The questions of what he should do about the girl, about Knight's crime. His proof had been taken; who would believe him now? A battered and failing journalist's word against that of the greatest politicians this country had ever seen.

The door opened slightly and someone entered the room. Bare feet padded across the floorboards towards the bed. Normally he would have been slightly alarmed at the sound of an intruder, reality drawing him back out of his semi delirious move to sleep, but this time he was too shattered to care. The shadow moved to the bed and leaned over him. He felt the edge of the tartan woollen blanket brush against his face.

"It's only me, don't panic," Ludvine's voice whispered in the darkness. Without another word, she set herself on the other side of the mattress, rolling over so that she could look at him, the blurred outline just visible in the darkness. He could sense her intent gaze, as if expecting him to suddenly do something. Nothing happened.

"It's uncomfortable on the floor down there," she said, not knowing if he was awake. She paused, listening closely, and when she got no response, she presumed he must have passed out as soon as he had set his head on the pillows.

"I was nodding off."

A crack moved up the mattress as she stretched her body out full length on the bed. With his eyes closed, his senses were more highly tuned, the sounds of the night loud in his ears. He felt the air shift as she moved up close against him, the sensation of her light breath on the side of his face. Unexpectedly, she kissed him on the cheek, before swiftly rolling onto her back as if embarrassed by what she had just done.

"Sorry," she whispered to no one in particular.

"Don't be," he replied to the dark. He heard the sound of her hair moving against the sheet as she twisted her head to look over at him. It was the mere action that was important, despite the fact that neither of them could see very much in this poor light. If he left the situation as it was now, it would be ignored tomorrow. They would both pretend that there had been nothing, there would be the awkward mindless conversation about the weather, Ludvine would depart and that would be the conclusion. He would leave the village, take a mediocre newspaper job somewhere and they would never see each other again. Now and then they would think about that strange character they had met by chance in the little northern village all those years ago, wondering what had happened, what the other one was doing now. Because there would be no doubt that they would be doing something interesting. They had seemed like such special people. What ifs and missed opportunities always did offer fascinating lifestyles, especially in retrospect.

He had to force himself to move. Every joint in his body had rusted and seized up. His body wanted to rest, to sleep. His mind wanted Ludvine. He ran a hand down the side of her face. Her skin was smooth, warm, somehow secure. The mere fact that she really was there beside him seemed to take the anxiety away. He kissed her, uncertainly brushing his lips up against hers, at first not sure where exactly he would land. Ludvine kissed back, gently, as if afraid of hurting him.

Her fingers moved over the top of his sweater, tracing his collar bone. "You should sleep."

Aran settled back down, staring up at the ceiling. He body sank into the bed, nearing slumber. Ludvine pulled the blanket a little more tightly around her shoulders and rolled onto her side, hunched up against him. She rested her head against his shoulder. He could feel strands of her soft hair against his face. Ludvine. He closed his eyes.

He woke with a start, bursting through the long tirade of nightmares. Blinking in the crisp morning light, he could not remember what had happened. The pain swiftly reminded him as he shifted position. His body like robust cardboard, inflexible and designed on purpose to stubbornly remain in one shape. A dull ache returned to his right leg as he bent his knee. The worst came from his jaw. Even memories could cause discomfort. Recollections of the beating, of Mildew bent over him plucking out the remains of a shattered tooth, the blood, the pain, Ludvine's worried expression, sitting in the darkness in front of a lunatic mathematician's house, flicking his tooth away into a pool of black. Even the macho shame, supposedly dying out in these times of the modern man. Aran squeezed his eyes shut.

Sitting up, he forced himself to acknowledge reality. Glancing across the bed, he caught sight of Ludvine's sleeping figure, remembering more pleasant episodes from the previous night. Like himself, she was still fully dressed. Unconscious, curled up in the foetal position with the red tartan blanket pulled tight around her body. For a moment he wondered if it really was Ludvine.

Like a cripple, he stiffly swung his legs over the side of the bed and set his feet down on the rough, untreated floorboards. Every time he moved his right leg he could feel a slight pain crack through his shin.

He walked over the landing to the half-renovated bathroom to make an appraisal in the mirror. The board he had fixed to the window when the room had been a makeshift dark room was now stood in the corner where they would probably put the toilet if they ever finished the renovations. Grey light came in through the window and the sound of rain pattered against the glass.

Setting his right foot on the edge of the bath, he pulled up the trouser leg to inspect the damage. A bruise was only just starting to form. Staple's well-aimed kick to his leg must have been powerful, and he supposed he would carry the mark for a few weeks like a brand. A putrid coloured declaration he had not been capable of defending himself.

A tinge in his lower jaw distracted him. He turned to the mirror where Ludvine had pulled her tooth out a couple of nights ago. Peering into the sink, which he had not touched since witnessing her gruesome behaviour, he was surprised to see that the discarded tooth and blood splatters were gone. As if she had never been here extracting teeth. Of course she had not pulled out teeth, she was sleeping in his bed at this very moment with a full set in her mouth. He must have dreamt the entire episode. It was just that it had been so vivid.

A glance in the mirror presented a face not quite as bad as he had been preparing himself for. Now that the blood had been washed away, he almost looked respectable. There was swelling around his lower jaw due to the dental work. Mildew had told him that it would go down in a couple of days. Apart from that there was bruising on the skin, which must have been the point of impact of Staple's shoe. The final conclusion: he was dishevelled and battered but still standing.

Continuing the check, his eyes ran over his hands, which were scratched and rough-edged from being dragged across gravel. There were also marks of kicks and punches as he had held up his hands in self-defence. Blotches of light bruising showed up in patches. Pulling up his sweater and shirt, both baggy items these days, he winced as he saw the violently coloured bruising on the side of his torso. That was not attractive and of all the wounds looked the most dramatic at present. Now that he was examining it, acknowledging its existence, it seemed to hurt more. It had lain dormant through the night but it was now awake and demanding attention.

"That's not a pretty sight."

Aran looked up sharply, dropping his shirt. He had forgotten that he was not alone in the house. He had grown accustomed to solitude years ago. He would often forget that there actually were other people in the world. Ludvine was leaning against the doorframe. The blanket hung loosely around her shoulders, sweeping down to the floor. Her face was clear this morning, noticeably pale. Without the heavy eyeliner, she looked innocent, almost angelic had it not been for the curious little spark in her eyes.

"Does it hurt?" she asked, stepping into the room.

"A bit, but I'll survive," Aran responded, already feeling a gnawing ache along the length of his jaw from his first words of the day. "I don't know if I'm going to be able to eat much for a while though."

Ludvine smiled without humour, a sad, sympathetic look. "You'll be on liquids for a little while, I guess. It's not every day you get your teeth kicked out." Her shoulders sagged and distress crept upon her. "Jesus, I still can't believe this actually happened. Does this happen to you a lot with your job?"

Aran smiled wryly as he lowered his body onto the edge of the bath. "Not as often as you might think. I've only had three real thrashings before, but this is the worst..." He drifted off, not really wanting to discuss it. It did not seem very heroic, or particularly manly to admit to having been beaten up. Twice he had suffered for his work, the first time could have been avoided had it not been for his inexperience as a journalist. A little more tact would have saved him. The third episode had actually been a by-product of living in London. The statistics were bound to catch up with you in some way in areas so concentrated in human population. It had been a mugging by a couple of youths. He had taken the punches and accepted the bruising. Staple's beating had been the worst for the simple fact that Aran had not been able to fight back at all. It was pathetic in so many ways, merely collapsing on the ground and taking what Staple had decided he deserved.

"What are you going to do now?" Ludvine gingerly placed herself on the edge of the bath. She wanted to reach out and touch him, but now that the mystery of the night was lost, she honestly did not know where she stood with Aran.

"About this? Wait until it all heals. As for Staple, there's nothing I can do. His word against mine."

"And the girl?"

Aran lowered his eyes. He did not really care anymore. The story was lost and he did not know the girl. Rachel Applegate had had her chance to escape that day when he had been driving out of the property. He was too jaded to save the world these days. "There's not a lot more I can do now. I have no evidence. I gave the pictures to Staple. It's just one beaten up journalist against one the greatest politicians this country has ever had."

"The pictures, of course," Ludvine mumbled, averting her eyes and turning to the bath tub for something to look at. The grubby white tub was covered in a layer of photographs depicting architecture, presumably Knight's family home. The photographs were impressive, the clarity and the angle, the composition of the images. He did not seem to care, these pictures absently tossed into the bath as if they were scrap paper worthy only of dust sheet status. She picked up one picture, glancing over the form of the stone circle they had visited together, before dropping the image back into the dry bath. "These are very good," she sighed, wondering why he wasted this talent. Not that she knew anything about making advantage of talent. "But you must have negatives." She looked up sharply. "You didn't give those to Staple, now did you?"

"No, but they're gone," he confessed. "I noticed last night when we got back. He must have broken into the cottage; my negatives were all over the kitchen. No doubt the one I need has been taken." He shrugged to himself. "So there's no evidence."

"And your story?"

"Essentially finished. There's not much else I can do with it now."

Ludvine nodded slowly. "So there's not much else to do except pack up and move on."

"That's pretty much it, but..." he broke off, watching her melancholy stare at the floor. But he did not want to leave, despite everything. It seemed like a weakness to say that he wanted to stay a little longer because of one person. To say that he wanted to reorganise a life, a way of existing because someone within his current circle of contact had sparked an interest. Ludvine raised her head slowly, gradually meeting his eye. Impulsively, he reached forward, his hands against her skin as he kissed her. Ludvine meeting him half way across the gap. They toppled backwards, sliding down against the smooth enamel wall of the bath and landing on the layers of photographs. Ludvine twisted around. She was almost crawling over the pictures, her fingers caught up in his hair as she took the warmth of his mouth. His neck rested against the corner of the bath by the taps, legs hanging over the side, arms pulling Ludvine down on top of him. Her hands became almost erratic, engulfed by passion, and reaching out at the air, unconscious of what they were doing. Her fingers came up against the taps, and her palm pressed up against the metal. Aran let out a gasp as the cold water suddenly poured out into the bath, seeping into his clothing.

Startled, Ludvine pulled back, quickly turning off the tap. "Sorry, I wasn't thinking about what I was doing," she said, sitting back on her legs. There was a thin covering of cold water disappearing down the plug hole, wet photographs stuck to the surface. She broke out into a smile. "Maybe this isn't the best place to be."

Aran laughed. "You have to improvise. This place is a bit empty."

"Back to basics," Ludvine mused. "Do you have any food here? My stomach thinks my throat's been cut."

"Sure." Aran pulled himself out of the bath. "Let's go downstairs. You can eat and I can find some dry clothes."

Ludvine spent the remainder of the morning cross-legged on the floor in the packed chaos of the living room. She had found a box of Aran's jumbled photographs and poured over the images for hours, fascinated.

"It's like you've documented every moment of your life," she spoke, moving through the years, buildings, events, landscapes, people. "Yet you don't appear in a single picture." She paused mid way through a collection of black and white photographs taken outside a huge circus tent, flicking through performers coming out from the show or waiting to go in.

"I suppose you're going to put some psychological twist on that now," Aran joked as he sat down, a mug of freshly brewed tea in his hand. "I go through life without participating."

"I wouldn't say that," Ludvine responded. "What about those bruises? You certainly participate in life. It's just that you don't seem to feature anywhere here, as if you don't consider yourself important enough…" She stopped and laughed. "Although I'm no psychologist and I'm certainly in no position to criticise."

Aran wondered what she was thinking as she turned her attention back to the images. "It's the nature of my work," he spoke, wishing he dared to photograph her now. The gentle light coming through the windows gave a soft glow around her figure, her tangled hair tied loosely off her face. Her eyes seemed smaller without the make up, yet more beautiful, ethereal. "Writing, photography. It's just observing the world and communicating it back to people."

"When people let you," Ludvine muttered as she flicked through the pictures. "Oh, look at the clowns!" she exclaimed, suddenly bursting out into laughter. "This guy looks like Bill." She looked over at him. "You know Bill, the landlord at the Fox and Hound?"

Aran nodded.

"I remember when I moved back from Denmark last year, I came back on the day of the village fete, the year they got Bill to dress up for the kids. The local organisers had been on at him for years to do it. It was so funny, dressed up like a clown. He hated it of course, swore he'd never do it again, and that you can believe. You'd have to have him at gun point for a repeat performance."

"Why did you come back from Denmark? I mean, this is a beautiful area, nice little village, but beyond the cleaning there doesn't seem to be much to do."

Ludvine smiled sadly. "That old thing," she sighed. "Denmark was something to do whilst I figured out my life. I love it; I have family there, but still I don't feel like I belong permanently... I missed home, the countryside or something I guess. I suppose I was looking for something when I moved over there, but I never found it. I probably never will. I don't know what I'll do. I can't stay here forever. It feels stunted, stagnant. I love it too; it's where I grew up, but it feels like time never moves, like everything's jumbled." She set the photographs down. "I can't say there's really anything holding me here apart from the fact that I don't really have anywhere to go, anything to do. Maybe I'm like your pictures, just observing, but never living, never experiencing."

"If this is the effect, then we're putting the pictures back in the box." Aran took the photographs from her hands and tossed them back in with the masses swarming in the cardboard box. He could understand what she was trying to explain, but had no real concrete words of advice, nothing to solve the problem. The dilemmas of modern, western living. There was no simple answer. He wished he could make it better for her. "Shit, after the past day I have had, I can't get onto the meaning of life..."

"All those serious and depressing thoughts," Ludvine joked as she stretched back on the floor. Resting her head on her arms, she gazed up at the ceiling. "I suppose all of that is really beyond human comprehension. If there is a point to it all of course." Her eyes flittered back to Aran, sitting by her side drinking tea.

"I didn't realise you were a philosopher."

"Oh yes," she joked. "I'm a jack of all trades, you'd be surprised."

The mug was drained. Aran put it to the side and turned to her. "Do you have to work today?"

"Work?" Ludvine scoffed. "I'm looking for work, that's about it." She set her lips together, listening to the gentle sound of the drizzle against the thin panes of glass in the French windows. She looked back at him. "Why?"

"No reason." Aran replied evasively as he leaned across her body, moving up towards her face. Despite his recent war wounds, he was feeling quite nimble, his body propped up against the hard floor. Beside Ludvine. She accepted him, taking him down with her. Outside it began to rain heavier, the colours of nature enriched and more vivid, the hues of tree bark, stone and earth strengthened. The scent of rainfall was thick in the air all day.

Aran drove Ludvine back to the village in the late afternoon when the rain had ceased. At the edge of the village green, she hopped out of the car onto the damp grass, blades drenched in rain water brushing against the long legs of her trousers. She smiled at him, his own happiness reflected in her face, and she swept around to stalk across the expanse of grass to the far side.

Now alone, he lacked any desire to return to the cottage, yet was simultaneously keen to avoid the village both out of shame and a sense of banishment. He did not want people to see the bruise on the side of his face. Opening the glove compartment, a corner crammed with jumbled papers, books, camera films and other things that just might come in useful one day, he pulled out the rough tourist map and spread it out across the steering wheel. The stone circle and the Knight estate he had seen, with no desire to return. That resounding deep sense of failure. There were still other local features he had yet to explore, and he settled on the lake as a suitable diversion for what was left of the afternoon.

A small winding road twisted through a well-established broadleaf forest, traversing down a gentle bank to the side of the lake. Where water met land a bare patch of earth grudgingly functioned as car park. It was empty, and stepping out of the car into the peaceful atmosphere of the lakeside forest, it seemed as if the entire world was sleeping. He could understand what Ludvine meant when you said you could get lost in this place; it was hard to believe the rest of the world was still out there.

The standard background sound of bird chatter filtered through the trees; the birds themselves concealed by the thick, glowing green foliage of the trees. Water lapped lazily up against the shore, a sound almost willing him into an absent slumber.

Slinging the camera over his shoulder, he started out on the earthen track that sauntered along the edge of the water. When he stopped for a moment, concentrating on the air, he realised that he could not even hear the incredibly faded drone of traffic. There were probably few places left in England where such an escape from modern urban living was possible. It reminded him of his early childhood out on the Shetlands, despite the dramatic difference in terrain.

Twigs snapped as something moved within the forest up ahead. Turning from the view of the water, he peered forward, catching sight of fleeting signs of movement. Stepping out from behind the trees obstructing his view, he watched a figure stagger onto the footpath, having just run down the steep bank. Despite the heavy covering of clothing, baggy and functioning as a disguise of body, the arms were bare and revealed the general physical emaciation. Arms like bone with loose pale skin, it was like watching a living skeleton. The figure was wearing a long, misshapen dress, once white, now an ugly grey, crying out for a wash. The skirts were particularly stained, dark heavy blocks like watermarks from a rising tide. It was hard to guess what had left those rust coloured stains. Aran started forward but stopped as the figure twisted to meet his gaze.

Ludvine stood in the path ahead of him. This was not the Ludvine he had left barely half an hour ago. She had dropped in weight to a terrifying degree. Her body was a mere moving collection of weakening bones. Her face was hollow and sickly pale, her eyes sucked back into her skull leaving great shadows on the surface. Long hair was in ill repair, hanging in thick lumps, dirty and unwashed for weeks. She looked positively ill, and it seemed a mere miracle that in such a state she was still able to walk without difficulty. Her mouth opened and he could hear her rasping breath. The tooth that he had thought he had dreamt her pulling was missing, as was one of her front teeth and another from the lower jaw. Only in her twenties, yet she resembled an old hag, a former shadow of a human being.

This was not possible. He had just seen Ludvine thirty minutes ago. She had been full of youth, well-kept and at a healthy weight. This creature was a wretch, but she was also definitely Ludvine. Previous theories of insanity, whilst probably applicable for what he now saw, were not relevant for the girl who had been in his bed this morning. They could not be the same person and yet they were one and the same. Ludvine had been adamant that she had no siblings, no twin sister. A theory of madness, a split personality did not work with the evidence anymore, for this dramatic change in appearance and health in such a short period was not possible. There had to be a sister, a sister that Ludvine herself was unaware of. It was the only logical explanation.

Ludvine turned away from him, surprisingly nimble, scampered away down the path like a forest creature. The dress, several sizes too large for her billowed like a ship's sail.

Aran hung in dumb silence. "Ludvine?" he spoke quietly, still bewildered. His mind snapped back to the speed of reality. "Wait!" he called out into the forest, but she did not hear. He hurried after her.

Ludvine followed the path for a short distance before suddenly diving off the track and dragging her frail form through the forest, randomly slipping between trees, a zig zag course that seemed definite despite her erratic movements. Aran followed, surprised at how fast he had to move to keep up. He stumbled out into a small clearing. There was a large dank hole, nearing a meter deep, cutting the otherwise perfect flow of the forest. Ludvine was on her hands and knees, scrabbling in the dirt and digging like an animal. Grains of soil flew into the air behind her, a fountain of mud, catching in her hair, splattering into the surrounding grass.

Aran felt sick watching her. He had to remind himself that this was not Ludvine. This was the secret sister, a notion that sounded as ridiculous as the soap operas it had appeared on in such serious capacity. It was the best he could come up with.

She paused for a moment, peering into her hole, perhaps a prepared grave, before returning to digging, even more furiously as if she had found what she was looking for. Either that or she was almost ready. Ready for what?

Aran stood at the edge of the clearing, unable to do anything, too shocked by what he had discovered. Ludvine stopped digging, like a little dog that had finished for the day, and turned around, knowing instinctively that he was stood close by watching her. Her dull, lifeless little eyes stared intently up at him. "Come and look," she requested. The lunatic did speak.

Apprehensively he approached the hole. Perhaps she was planning to kill him, before filling in her hand made burial plot. She was hardly threatening though, and he could easily over power her if necessity called. As he moved closer, the mouth of the hole seemed to grow wider. He stopped at the edge and stared down, wishing he had never come to the lake.

There was a human body in that dank grave, revealed by Ludvine's dirty hands. The corpse was in an advanced state of decay, certainly beyond recognition; flesh had rotted, or at least had been eaten away. There were black holes in the head where eyes had once been, the open mouth filled with teeth that were stained by the earth. Ludvine had only excavated the head and neck to a well-worked degree, the suggestion of the rest of the body starting to rise forth from the earth. There was a heavy stench of decay, of putrid flesh. He had no comprehension of how long it had been here, but he would have guessed at weeks, if not months.

Aran had learned a little about pathology from pestering forensic officers at crime scenes and reading up on the subject to give his writing a little more knowledgeable flair. The decay of bodies was generally a miscomprehension in the public mind. People seemed to think that a body would rot to clean white bones within days sometimes, but the process of decay was a many varied system, dependant on so many different factors. He could remember parts of an article he had read a long time ago about the decay of animal matter, how a body in earth took longer than one discarded on ground surface. Even then the time varied to extreme degrees depending on depth, temperature, soil type and other factors. Even the state of the corpse before death played a role: a murder or accident victim taking longer than say someone who had been sick for a long time prior to death.

His eyes moved back to Ludvine, who was still crouched on the forest floor, unperturbed by what she had just dug up with her bare hands.

"You did this?" he asked.

She shook her head at him. Her cognitive system apparently still worked enough for her to understand the charge and declare herself innocent. For the first time, this shroud-clad, distorted skeleton spoke to him with more than a couple of words. "I didn't do it," she said, her voice somewhere between a whisper and a plea. "He did it, don't you know? He did it. I saw him."

She turned back to the cadaver, reaching out to it and running her hand down to the side of what remained of the rotting face. Aran shuddered in disgust.

"She was only young. Poor thing, poor thing."

He had to draw himself out of this gruesome disconnected observation. A body had been found in the woods; the authorities would have to be informed. He stared at Ludvine's back. She seemed to know what had happened, yet had not reported it. Too deluded now to understand the formalities of civilised society. "Murder?"

She nodded. "Murder. He did it." She turned her head as he crouched down beside her. Her eyes were haunting, yellow orbs pushed back in shadows. "It was the other one."

"The other one what?"

"The other one!" She stared up at him, her eyes urgent.

What was she talking about?

"There were two in the beginning… the other one."

"Then there was one," Aran finished for her. He started down at the corpse, surprised at how calm he was. The immediate horror had subsided as if he was looking at a wax model, as if none of this was real. Who was she?

"Brought her down from the big house when she was dead and buried her here," Ludvine continued. "I followed."

The big house. Aran's eyes widened. "Knight?" he spoke out the name, aghast.

Ludvine nodded her confirmation.

A young girl lying in her secret grave. There had been two and now there was one. Rachel Applegate had been with a friend the day she disappeared. A friend who was missing too, but he had never wondered what had happened to her. That logically they ought to be in the same place. The most probably conclusion. Rachel Applegate and Tanya Cole. First there were two and now there was one.

Tanya had been spared further suffering. She had been dead for months. She had escaped Knight, been permitted to flee from existence. The truth about Knight was even worse than he had first thought. It was no surprise that Knight had Staple working for him.

Rachel Applegate was still alive. He had kept one and extinguished the other as if she were an unwanted toy. Why would he do that? If it were for the pleasure of killing, then why was Rachel still alive at all after all this time? Had the murder been performed in order to terrify the girl, to make sure that she would not dare escape.

"Do you know why he did this?"

"She was no use. The other one worked faster, once she was ready, he didn't need her."

"Once she was ready?" She was talking in riddles, the garbled nonsense of a mad woman. Perhaps he could not rely on anything she told him. "Rachel was ready first? Ready for what?"

Ludvine actually looked surprised. "Don't you know? Don't you understand?" she asked, not waiting for an answer. "They all did it. He's doing it now."

"Doing what?"

"The graves," she whispered hoarsely. "Didn't you see the graves? The answer's with the dead."

"The graves? What do you mean? Ludvine, can't you just give me a straight answer?" Aran pleaded with her, desperate to know the truth. Ludvine stood up and stepped away from the hole.

"Do you mean the Knight family plot?" he asked, recalling that strange long line of headstones, one after the other. They were only graves, even if the lay out had been a little odd. There had been nothing there that would explain this. He turned back to look at Tanya's corpse, as if she would suddenly come to life, sit up and explain it to him. He had his proof now, he thought to himself on a side track. The photos were gone, but a body buried in the woods was always much more convincing.

"Ludvine, when did this all happen?" he asked, turning once again to look at that shallow, dying face, but she was no longer there. She must have crept away whilst he was looking at the murder victim, for he was alone in the woods.

Aran was not sure what distressed him more: finding Tanya Cole's decayed remains or Ludvine the deranged crone. The wretch could not possibly be Ludvine. Identical biologically, still, it could not be her. Like a mirror image of the woman if things went wrong. He was unnerved to recall that she had actually responded to the name Ludvine. It had to be some family relation, either one that Ludvine was ignorant to or one that was a family embarrassment and not spoken of. It all sounded too Victorian to be viable.

Ludvine's crazed rambling about the answer being in the graves echoing on repeat in his immediate memory, he followed the track worn into the earth by many feet to the church. Silence dominated the churchyard.

Aran stood beside the elongated, self-contained family plot behind the church. It was, as Ludvine had pointed out to him the other day, exclusively male: a long line of fathers and sons stretching back across the past few hundred years. Aran travelled forward in time until he reached the final grave, that of Patrick Knight's father. Tilting his head, he considered the sparse information. Albert Knight, born 12 June 1902, died 2 March 1954. He had not really lived that long, only just making it past his fiftieth birthday. Knight himself had grown up without a father, a fact Aran was already aware of, but seeing the elder man's grave brought reality forth snapping. Knight's father must have passed away just after he was born. Aran could not remember the exact date of Patrick Knight's birth off hand, but he knew that it was sometime in the fifties. He wondered what that did to a person, growing up without a father figure. Would that be Knight's excuse for his disgraceful behaviour? It was pathetic to think in such terms, because there were, had been, and always would be millions of people living out their childhood without any example of a father, and they had gone on to be decent ordinary people. There was no excuse for the acts he had committed.

Information for murders could not be hidden in graves the way Ludvine had suggested. Not burials this old. She must have fantasised the entire conspiracy. Mentally unstable, unbalanced, dysfunctional Ludvine. Aran sighed to himself, ready to give up. There was nothing here except an odd family tradition of burying the men in a long line. Arrogant, full of self-importance and fuelled by vanity, but it did not explain murder.

Murder, of course. The thought in his mind stepped forward from the recesses. He had been so concerned with solving the full stretch of Knight's guilt, that he had neglected to consider the reality of the situation. A body had been discovered in a shallow grave in the woods. He had no proof as to how she had died, but plausible explanations that did not include murder were sparse. The police would have to be notified.

Aran felt his stomach knot up, the bruising on his shin starting to throb. He could taste the blood in his mouth again. The fury of Staple's malice, the threats, the words, lurching warnings. He could hardly turn up at Staple's door and report that he had found the body of Tanya Cole. Besides which, Staple probably already knew about it. Perhaps he had even helped Knight to dispose of the body. Aran would have to call out of the village, get in touch with some kind of national help line for the case, or at worst the missing person's department, although he had no proof that the body was that of Tanya Cole. Only his gut feeling and demented chatter from an insane woman.

Aran began to slowly move, his eyes drifting over the next grave. Patrick Knight's grandfather, Gregory Knight, born 12 December 1849, died 13 June 1902. He had not lived that long either, just passing fifty. Perhaps the family had a hereditary condition of a weak heart or fragile constitution that up until now had not been controlled by modern medicine. Patrick Knight certainly did not look ill.

The following grave was that of his great grandfather. Edmund Knight, born 24 August 1799, died 12 December 1849.

Aran halted, peering closely at the date of death. Taking a long step backwards, he reappraised Edmund's son's grave, that of Patrick's grandfather. Edmund had died the same day as his son had been born. The exact same day. Bad luck. Another Knight who never got to know his father.

Returning to the most recent grave, Patrick's father, he considered the date of birth. Albert had been born on the 12 June 1902. His father, Gregory, had died on the 13 June 1902. The day after. And like the other two he had only lived into his early fifties. Health conditions were plausible, exact dates for death timed with the birth of children were not family traits. If men could give birth maybe, but as it stood, this seemed too odd to be coincidence.

The crumbling grave of Patrick's great great grandfather. This man, a certain Charles Knight had been born on the 2 November 1757 and had died on the 24 August 1799. That same day, his son, Edmund Knight had been born. Aran moved backwards along the graves, unable to remember all the relevant dates. Edmund had lived until the 12 December 1849, the same day as the birth of his son Gregory. Gregory had died the day after the birth of his son Albert. Albert was born on the 12 June 1902; Gregory had died on the 13 June 1902.

The probability of this happening by random chance was incredibly small. What exactly had the Knight family been doing? It could be completely irrelevant of course, but perhaps Ludvine was not quite as mad as first appearances suggested. A translation of the graveyard was needed.

His thoughts returned to the library he had seen in Knight's home. There would be masses of papers and diaries left by his ancestors, comments and explanations to this odd lineage. Perhaps the reasons. There was no chance

Aran was going to gain access to those precious volumes now.

Aran hurried out of the graveyard and headed back for his car. Staggering out onto the back lane, he noticed Ludvine emerging from the community centre. She was wearing a long turquoise skirt with a wide darker blue sash covered in lines of small silver coins. The length of her back was exposed, her upper body in a long-sleeved, cropped top. Her hair was loose and slightly wind blown. She slung her coat over her arm as she bent forward to lock up the doors.

Dropping the keys into a cloth bag full of CDs, she picked up the bag by the thin handles, and turned to leave. Aran stopped in the middle of the lane so that she would notice him and hopefully approach. She looked stunning in full costume. Her eyes were intense as she watched him, the usual heavy black outlining in place, with the addition of a rich blue hue brushed over the remainder of her eyelids. She must have been teaching one of her belly dancing classes. She had not mentioned it earlier when he had given her a lift back into the village.

She nodded to him casually. "Been hanging around the graveyard again?"

"I just needed to check something out," he responded, the urgency of the Knight mystery beginning to fade as his concentration took a new focus. "I was actually down at the lake earlier."

Ludvine looked bored but she managed to feign an interest. "Oh? It's nice down there. Well, I'd…"

"I saw someone down there," Aran interrupted her, not sure how to tell her about the odd woman who had taken him to Tanya Cole's grave. "I actually thought it was you at first, but it couldn't have been…"

Ludvine gave him a curious stare. "It certainly wasn't. I've been working all day," she said it as if honest work was beyond him. Aran ignored the bitter hint and continued.

"She is the spitting image of you, but she's ill, you just have to look at her to know that." He paused, watching for a telling reaction. If she knew about a crazy relative running wild in the woods, she did not show it. She was incredibly calm. Either she did not know or she simply did not care. "Do you have any relatives that…"

"Jesus, you are unbelievable!" Ludvine burst out furiously, her eyes flashing, the anger all the more apparent from the emphasis of her make up. "Whenever I see you, you're thinking of some bizarre way to insult me. I am not mad, I do not pull my teeth out and I do not have a crazy twin sister living in the forest if that's what you're thinking of starting on now. You want to get your article written and bugger off because I am sick of bumping into you and having to listen to this crap."

"Come on, Ludvine, calm down," he said, trying to make the peace. "I'm not trying to offend you and I'm sorry if it seems like that. I'm just concerned."

"You're just screwed in the head." Ludvine threw back curtly. "Every time I see you…"

"Every time?" Aran laughed at her accusation. "It's hardly that often. I thought we were getting on, I thought…"

"Hardly that."

"Let's not fight, this isn't worth it." He moved to embrace her, but Ludvine sensed what he was about to do, and darted out of reach. There was an odd look of fear in her eyes. She did not want to show it, preferring or needing to put up a cover of strength. What had happened in the past couple of hours? Her mood had changed violently. If he had mentioned it this morning, he guessed she would have just laughed the matter off.

"I'm going home," she muttered. "I'd prefer it if you'd leave me alone if you see me again."

"Ludvine! Why are you being like this? I think we should talk about this. We could go back to your place…"

"No!" She looked utterly horrified at the suggestion. "Just leave me alone."

She hurried away, fleeing a wild and unpredictable animal. The coins on her sash jingled, almost mocking as her figure virtually ran down the lane. Aran was left in bewilderment. What had just happened? It had been as if she had completely forgotten everything that had happened last night, this morning. She had looked at him as if he was mad. Perhaps it was not Ludvine's mental state that needed the attention.

Something tapping on the living room windowpane brought him out of the distant consciousness. As if guilty of a crime, he swiftly gathered up the photographs – Knight's estate, Ludvine by the stone circle, local images of recent moments - and stuffed them into the back of a kitchen cupboard. He did not wish to repeat the previous mistake of Rachel Applegate's photograph. People were very rarely to be trusted. He didn't even try to rationalise why anyone would want to steal his remaining inoffensive pictures.

Ludvine's figure stood outside the locked doors, peering into the shabby living room. He was surprised to see her. She had said she did not want to see him yet she now came out of the village specifically to visit him. It made little sense, but she would have an explanation, he supposed. No longer the Egyptian dancer, but a normal woman, dressed in jeans that were so long that they dragged behind her heels as she walked. Aran twisted the key in the lock and opened the door.

"Hi there," Ludvine started, growing cautious as she noted the distinctly cool expression on his face. "I'm not interrupting anything am I?"

Aran shook his head. "Come in if you want. As long as you're not going to start a fight."

"Oh right." Ludvine spoke, presuming that he had been arguing with an editor over the phone or something of that nature. "Who have you been fighting with this afternoon?"

Aran could not hold back the laugh of bewilderment. "You."

"Me?" She sounded confused. "Did we fight this morning? I thought we got on quite well."

It was a convenient lapse of memory. Maybe she was embarrassed for over reacting, or perhaps she wanted to avoid all reference to the strange woman in the woods. "This afternoon," he reminded her, not intending to pretend that it had never happened. "I don't know what was up. You seemed afraid of me."

Ludvine walked over to him. "What are you talking about? I didn't see you this afternoon."

"What, so your twin sister did? Or your triplet rather?"

Ludvine laughed, his comment was slightly amusing, and besides, there seemed to be little else to do. She had no idea what had upset him. "You know I'm an only child. Maybe you're concussed or something."

"You're telling me that we didn't speak outside the community centre a couple of hours ago? You'd just been teaching a class."

"A class?" She raised her eyebrows.

"Jesus, Ludvine," he burst out, impatiently irritated with her. "What are you doing to me? You keep denying having spoken to me, screwing with my head like this. I can't be going mad, so what is it?" Famous last words, he thought afterwards. The possibility that he was going mad was not an option. There was nothing wrong with him. He was sane.

Ludvine pursed her lips, not sure how to respond. "I'm sorry, I'm not doing anything on purpose. But I swear to God, I haven't seen you all afternoon, not since you dropped me off in the village." She paused, calmly considering him. "Do you think you might be concussed? I mean, maybe you might be confusing today with another day."

He slouched down on top of a box of books and looked up at her. "And I might be going mad."

Ludvine broke out into a warm smile, as if they had broken through the stalemate and there was nothing more to be concerned about. "No. Just don't take it too seriously. I guess you'll be stressed, considering what you've found out about Knight and then Staple." She set herself down in his lap and lazily draped her arms around his neck. "There's nothing wrong with you," she assured him.

Aran was not convinced. He rested his head against her shoulder and gazed out of the window to the darkening skyline. Perhaps he never had spoken to Ludvine that afternoon. It was the product of a tired imagination. Either that or he was slowly sinking into insanity. If that much were possible, then how did he even know that Tanya Cole really was buried out in the forests by the lake? Or that the strange, dying skeleton version of Ludvine really existed? He was not sure that he knew what to believe anymore.

Whether he was mad or not, he could not leave Tanya Cole's disturbed cadaver to continue to rot in the forest. He had to report her murder. As he came up the farm track to the main road, the post box lying limply in the middle of the track forced him to halt the car. Picking the post box up, Aran noticed a hole in its side that he could not recall having seen before. As if the rusting metal had been punctured by a projectile. The post box was useless now, despite the fact that it had served no purpose prior to its demise. He tossed it back into the verge, not thinking of anything else to do with it.

At the cottage he hadn't been able to get any reception for his mobile. He drove to the village, glancing now and then at the screen in case the bars came up, which they never did. The telephone box by the village green was not working this morning either. There was a vacant lack of sound in the receiver. Aran had knocked on the pub door, waiting till Adele appeared, and had requested to borrow the telephone, explaining that the cottage where he was living was not connected, mentioning the mobile phone trouble. Adele had given her usual charming smile, before continuing to inform him that in fact the entire village had been disconnected this morning for maintenance work. She was not sure when the phone lines would be working again. Apparently it was hard to get any reception with most mobile phone networks in this area. The hills blocked off most signals.

He could not call out of the village and to inform the local police, and Constable Staple was worse than never reporting the crime at all. He still had to recover from the first beating. He was in no shape to step up for round two. He supposed he could keep driving until he came to a village where the telephones worked, and in many ways the thought of fleeing this place now felt like escape to paradise. But he was bound to this little village by invisible ties. The notion of leaving was almost comparable to falling off the edge of the world. A strange kind of agoraphobia. He couldn't bare to leave, and told himself it was perfectly acceptable to wait longer before informing the authorities of what had been unearthed.

He pulled out the tourist map. It was now tattered; the creases from where it had been folded up beginning to weaken, ready to break apart. There was a marked public footpath going out of the village at a westerly point, moving past fields, before approaching a forest and turning north. Here the path split and there were a couple of routes he could take including one that led up into the hills.

Aran was soon free of the village and out into the unrestricted countryside. His boot-clad feet strode across the earth, sweeping through windblown cascades of meadow grass and wild flowers. The trees were a darkened mass on the horizon, looming up against the brightly-lit meadow. The cover of branches and leaves provided sanctuary from the heat of the sun, which was creeping up to noon. Aran felt as if he was being baked alive within the shell of his clothes. It was a particularly sharp and intense day.

He halted on a wooden style, one foot on either side of the fence. The boundary marker formed a near perfect line stretching out along the length of the meadows and beyond in both directions. On the far side of the small meadow ahead began the forest. The change in vegetation was sharp and direct, simultaneous with a notable change in terrain. From the flat, rolling territory, the path rose up the steep banks of the gates to the forest, tree roots creeping up out of the sheer decline of earth.

A patch of movement caught his attention. A figure came up over the brink of another meadow, swinging around to climb into the forest. He quickly recognised the long hair, the shape of the body and the expected placing of character as that of Ludvine. He called out to her, waving his arms to try and draw her attention, but she did not hear him.

A second figure moved, as if having stepped out of the air itself. It was nothing so surreal, merely a change from stationary to motion but the sudden shift was unsettling. It was impossible to say who it was from this distance. The person soon scrambled into the forests after Ludvine. The choice of attire, the shapeless dark clothing transforming the human figure to little more than a blot.

People went walking alone in the countryside around here. Ludvine did it all of the time, even he was now. Seeing that second figure made him uneasy; the shapelessness was foreboding, warning of something off key with the natural balance. He was quite certain that the second figure and Ludvine were out walking independently of one another, yet there was a connection, something that would come to no good.

"Ludvine!" he shouted out at the forest, so loudly his lungs pushed against his ribs. He was beginning to feel nauseous, perhaps due to the sun. He started to run for the forest. The second figure vanished from view, swallowed up by the trees. Every step on the ground thudded through the soles of his feet, vibrating up the length of his spine like a heartbeat under pressure. The run dissolved out into a flat sprint, the wind resistance picking up and whipping against his face.

The forest bounced up into his near vicinity with speed as he ran to the line of outer trees. He scrambled blindly up the steep, rough path into the forest, not really stopping to wonder why he was suddenly so desperate, caught within such a deep panic. The sound of his own heavy breathing pulsated in his ears, blocking out the natural sounds of the forest. Twigs pulled against him like hands trying to delay his approach.

Inside the forest the pathway crumbled up into a confusing mess of narrow tracks, mere worn grooves in the forest floor, winding in all directions. The trees and bushes, underlying undergrowth, created a confusing backdrop. He could see neither Ludvine nor the stranger.

"Ludvine?"

He staggered to a halt, not sure in which direction he ought to run. Shadows flittered across the ground, over his flesh, the mottled patches of light against shadow, undefined edges, cast down through the net of leaves overhead. Inside the forest it was eerie, unsettling, watching and waiting.

There was a sound of movement up ahead, the noise of someone or something walking across the natural forest bedding of dead leaves and fallen twigs. "Aran?" She had heard him. Her voice sounded confused, uncertain. She had not been expecting to meet him out here in the forest. She was still invisible to him, her voice faded with distance as she stopped to listen deeper in the forest.

"Just wait where you are," he called back out to her, talking to the trees. "I'll soon catch up."

Ludvine did not respond. The forest was silent. Aran began to walk forward, having worked out roughly whereabouts Ludvine currently was from the direction of her voice.

"What do you want?" Her voice cut sharply with the question. Aran paused for a second as if thinking of a response, although it was obvious from the tone and the lowered volume that she was talking to someone else. She was talking to a person much closer, someone she could actually see.

"What are you doing carrying that thing around?" she asked, receiving no verbal reply that Aran could hear. "Oh no." Her words were a warning, steady in voice, an undertone of laughter sucked dry of humour. The second time she repeated the words, they were so different they could have been another language. Gone was the confidence, replaced by animal terror. She was no longer speaking, no longer guardedly warning, but instead screaming as if the amount of noise would stop the inevitable.

Aran started to run, twisting around the trees, flying forward desperate to reach her. Ludvine was screaming hysterically. Her cries echoed off the tree trunks, bouncing off at him from all directions to torment. It was disorientating to run through the forest in this state of panic. With every step he was faced with a repetition of the previous surroundings, the sound of Ludvine's fear moving through the mesh of branches.

Unexpectedly and abruptly her image appeared from between the trees. She was staggering forward, oblivious to the surroundings, gazing down in horror at her hands. Her bloodied fingers were held out in front, palms upwards as if she was begging for loose change but instead people would only spit blood at her. The white, long sleeved top she was wearing formed a stark contrast against the heavy dark blood stains splattered down the front of her torso. A deep gash through her porcelain flesh, the blood oozing as if being squeezed out of a tube. The blood was quite literally everywhere, dripping onto her shoes from her hands, from the wound, running down her arms, cast within the loose strands of her long hair like glistening beads.

Aran felt sick at the mere sight, appalled that she was suffering, wishing he could wipe it all away in a second. He ran towards her.

An arm suddenly appeared, attached to the figure he had seen, and a thick hunting knife plunged into Ludvine's abdomen. The sound held a nauseating resemblance to someone stabbing a knife into the body of a large watermelon. The sound of flesh, of liquid, of blood, everything plunging up against the metallic blade. Ludvine stopped walking, arching her back in pain on impact and leaning against the stranger who attacked from behind. A dark welt of blood swiftly spread out in the fabric of her clothing, reminiscent of ink blot tests from school years almost forgotten. The knife roughly dragged out of Ludvine's flesh and she staggered forward, gagging as if she was about to vomit.

Aran ran blindly at the attacker, throwing his shoulder into the dark clad body, pushing it away. Ludvine reached out to a tree trunk to stop herself falling, leaving a bloodied hand print on the bark.

The attacker hit Aran at the back of the head before pushing him away and onto the ground. Immediately dizzy, nauseous, unaware whether he was still standing or if he had fallen as he lay on the forest floor. The world was starting to move on its own accord. As he rolled onto his side, feeling the ache of the bruise on his torso courtesy of Staple begin to throb again, he looked up to see Patrick Knight standing a few metres away. Patrick was dressed in black, a large dark brown long sleeved shirt several sizes too big that hung impersonally on his body. A mottled flat cap pushed back on his head as if to disguise him from being recognised from behind. He stared down at Aran. A smile as if to say, 'now I have had my revenge. Now we are even'. The image began to flicker as if the forest was real but Knight was just a projected image, the product of poorly preserved film. Aran blinked and when he opened his eyes, Knight had gone. Pushing himself up onto his knees, he looked around to discover that Ludvine had also left the clearing.

They had not gone far. The sound of struggle against the forest fauna alerted him to their presence somewhere off to his right. He could hear Ludvine's voice, almost whimpering, weakly pleading, as she tried to fight back, but with the blood loss it was hardly an even contest.

"Ludvine," Aran spoke desperately as he staggered up onto his feet. There was a heavy blackness in his head, as if he were about to pass out.

Aran was not really looking where he was going as he rushed forward with the only thought of trying to save

Ludvine in his head. His foot caught on a tree root and he dived uncontrollably forward and downwards, crashing onto a bed of leaves and twigs with his arms grappling uselessly in front of him. He looked up just as Ludvine fell to the ground ahead. She must have tripped as well. He had to reach her and pull her away from danger. Protect her.

She was lying on her back, hair sprayed out against the hues of nature, the dry leaves, the brown earth and the patches of rich green moss. She gazed fearfully upwards as if she could see Knight lunge forward once again, the insane coward with his knife attacking an unarmed woman. Her mouth was hung partly open, as if holding her breath, wondering where this all would end.

Aran scrambled up onto his hands and knees and scuttled over to the distance of the last few remaining meters to where she lay. Knight must be psychopathic. But why Ludvine, why this cold blooded attack?

Ludvine!"

As he reached her side, he set his left hand on the ground, shuddering as it landed into something wet and slippery, still warm as if it had just escaped from the body. He glanced casually across, currently more concerned with Ludvine's still face, but swallowed down on his shock, the sickening feeling in the pit of his stomach as he saw what he had put his hand in.

Knight had gutted her like produce of a hunt. Aran looked back to her peaceful face. Despite the traces of terror, there was serenity upon her now. She was no longer was conscious of fear. Because she was no longer breathing. Because she was no longer trying to escape. Because she was dead. Her small and large intestine spilled out of her slashed abdomen like long bloodied eels lying in among the blades of grass, the natural forest refuse of dead leaves and twigs. The blood glistened from the specks of sunlight that made it through the canopy of foliage to the ground below. Her torso was thick with blood, deep dark red, slowly seeping outwards from the source with less speed now that the heart had ceased beating and there was only gravity left to guide the journey.

He looked around for Knight, but the man had disappeared. He was the only one in the forest, sat cowering over Ludvine's body. He had been too late. His shaking fingers, now covered in blood, hovered over her body, uncertain of what to do. His hands moved upwards, passing by her shoulders. For the first time Aran noticed that her neck had been slit, a fast and neat cut through her pale skin as if she had just brushed up against a pane of broken glass. He set his hand against the side of her face, smearing that perfect skin with her own blood. She was not going to wake up now. He could feel convulsions rippling through his body. This was not supposed to happen.

Aran knew the protocol, both of the police and of the journalist. The journalist should not get emotionally involved. As far as the crime scene was involved, both the journalist and the police could gain the most information if the items, the objects, the bodies were not interfered with. The scene was to be left as close to what it had been the moment the perpetrator had departed. They needed that link back to the chain of events. But Aran could not let be, picking her up by the shoulders and pulling her upper body so that he could cling to it, embrace it, as if that was all that was needed to make everything all right again. His body shook, clinging to her like the after effects of a shipwreck. Ludvine lay limp in his embrace, unresponsive. This was too real. It was no longer the story he wrote for the paper, about some woman, somewhere in the United Kingdom who had been butchered to death by an ex politician gone mad. This was someone he had known, someone perhaps he might have grown to love, or maybe he did already, he was too confused to really know.

It was completely silent. If he had been clearly thinking, he might have expected to hear the sound of Knight's retreating footsteps, but he was too focused on Ludvine. Or what had been Ludvine. It did not matter how much he clung to her body, for she would not come back to life. He could not bring himself to do anything else.

Aran stayed in the forest. Time in measured units became irrelevant. Now that he was lying in bed, he could not even remember getting up and driving back. He was just suddenly here. He could not recall what he had done with Ludvine, although he was reasonably certain that he had not told anyone what had happened. Every time he closed his eyes he saw her savaged body lying in the leaves. He felt as though he was going mad.

It was an obsession. He could think of nothing else. Sleep was impossible and when morning came he was still on his back, staring at the ceiling without actually seeing it. His brain was on overload and could not cope with outside stimuli. He was travelling within his mind. Sometimes he was happy, reliving the blissful moments with Ludvine. He told himself he had never experienced anything so right. He then recalled the confusion, the concern over her blips in memory, her strange behaviour. The run of thoughts always ended in the same way, trapped out in the forest, watching her die, holding her corpse in his arms. Panic would swell, as it became fresh once again that she was dead. He would choke, drowning in fresh country air. How could he possibly go on with life after this?

The day had passed by without notice, everything mixed up in confusion, stunted by grief. He could not even move on to the questions of what was he to do now. He was still trying to comprehend that she was dead. They had barely met, a few days, a week. A relationship still counted in hours.

He would sit for a minute and feel as though it had been days, take an hour between thinking he should stand up and actually performing the task, yet it felt like mere seconds. He was numb from his body. Existence was detached somewhere in the greater beyond. Frequently his mind was completely blank. Unaware of what day it was, where he was, what he thought he was doing here. It was a blessing for his traumatised brain, to gain a few respite periods when he could become separate from what he had witnessed.

As darkness began to sink steadily down to earth, so did his comprehension of reality. Bit by bit. Standing in the bathroom he had peered out of the window onto the rough grass. A scrubby patch eventually to be transformed into a garden when the renovations were complete. The moonlight flowed, so slowly sometimes he was sure he could see the paths the light beams took. Just as he was sure he saw Ludvine cross the garden like a ghost. She was thin, so painfully thin, wearing in that grimy, torn night dress, like a shroud. There was not a touch of breeze in the air as she had crossed the open land, her hair hanging rigidly.

His imagination could be cruel. He had turned away from the window, telling himself in a most convincing way that there was no one outside. He was too grief stricken to be thinking clearly. Lying down on the bed, he closed his eyes, and for the first time in the past forty-eight hours, he fell asleep.

He was in the forest again. Approaching the outer line of trees, the sound of his own breathing sharp inside his head. Beyond that, all sounds seemed muted and faded, as if he was underwater. His footsteps make no suggestion of movement as if walking on sponge. Ludvine was up ahead, the whiteness of the top she was wearing, had been wearing, glowing from the shade of the undergrowth. She disappeared and Aran was alone in the forest, circling in one place, searching for something familiar.

Ludvine screamed; the harsh, terrifying sound ripping through the stillness. It was incredibly distant, as if she was screaming down a tunnel. Aran started to run, pushing his way past trees, desperately trying to find her.

He stumbled upon the scene suddenly, although on approach no one had been lying at the foot of the tree.

Ludvine was dead. Her throat had been slit open and the fresh blood drenched her clothing. She lay on her back, arms spread out ungraciously across the bed of twigs and dead leaves, forest flowers watching on. There was a man hunched over by her side, his back to Aran. He was busy with the corpse, slitting open her abdomen as if preparing a recently shot deer for transportation home. No one wanted to carry all those internal organs. It would be forest carnage.

Aran felt as though he was about to vomit. Not again. He did not want to witness her murder again. And as the first time, he was too late to rescue her, too inept. There did not seem to be anything he was particularly worth while of these days.

With bloodied hands, the man pulled out the willing intestines, tossing them down onto the earth. As if sensing Aran's arrival, he abruptly halted his macabre work, and twisted around to look up at the new comer. Aran stared back in horror. He was looking at himself.

Suddenly he was running in the forest. It was a repetition of the previous trip, but now speeded up. Pressing fast forward, trying to get it over with. The first time he had walked, now he was running. Ludvine was running ahead, overwhelmed by panic. Aran had the hunting knife in his hand. Forcing himself to go faster, he caught up with his victim, slinging an arm around her chest from behind to pull her back to him. He plunged with the knife, as if to stab himself in the chest, but Ludvine was in perfect position to take the blow. He felt her body jolt as the cold metal cut through her flesh. Grinding against bone. The warm blood seeped up to the surface. Her hands went into spasm. He stabbed her again before flinging her weakening frame to the ground. She was crying, shaking, trying to think of the words that would persuade him not to continue. She had lost the power of speech. He was upon her, preparing to slit her throat and end this sobbing. He closed his eyes for a fleeting second, to summon the strength to take her life.

When he opened his eyes he was staring up at the darkened ceiling. He had killed Ludvine. He had seen in it his dreams. She was dead. Her blood was everywhere: running down the tree trunk, seeping out through the grains of dirt on the ground. He had killed her, had he not? He was suddenly filled with alternative explanations to the same result, the same ravaged corpse of Ludvine, but he could not remember which one was true. His mind felt as though it was crumpling. Perhaps he had killed her. Yet there was no motive. He had more reason to want her alive. She had made him happy. Now she was dead and he was sure he was going mad. Or perhaps the process had not only started but it was now complete. Had Ludvine not asked him once if he was mad? Maybe that was just his imagination as well.

He sat up and the sound of what seemed like hundreds of sheets of paper falling to the floor echoed through his silent room. A tidal wave shifting into consciousness. His bed was covered in glossy photographs. Many were cast across his legs as if the ceiling had opened up, rain clouds pouring photographs upon him. Utterly bewildered, Aran picked up one at random and peered at the image in the semi darkness. It was a picture of Ludvine, the one he had secretly taken when she had been dancing. Panic started to rise, and he scrabbled at the other photographs that were close at hand, his horror growing as he realised every image was of Ludvine.

This could not be possible, he had to be dreaming. He scrambled out of bed and fled for the light switch. Please, just take me back to reality. It was agony enough that Ludvine had been murdered, but for his imagination to start accusing him of the deed, that was to fall over the brink of the precipice and into insanity. Light could not be his saviour for all it revealed was the writing on the wall, quite literally the writing on the wall.

Obsession surrounded him in the objects that littered this room. It did not matter whether he was just in denial or innocent of the crime. Her name was everywhere, scrawled on the walls in thick blotchy letters as if it were the handwriting of a giant child. Aran reached out, feeling his stomach crunch in horror as his fingers touched the damp, red lettering on the wall. It might have been fresh paint of course, but it could also be blood. Either way, he did not know how it had come to be here. Intruders were the rational explanation but he could not think as to why anyone would do this. There was no logical reason. Only a madman would behave this way.

"I'm not mad." Aran whispered to himself. As if merely stating the fact would immediately eradicate the possibility. Gingerly pushing the door open, he peered out into the corridor. Her name was everywhere. Constant reminders, mocking and jeering. She is dead and there was nothing you can do to stop the course of events, to save her.

Someone had tied a red plastic bag to the post box. Billowing like a signal flag at the turn off onto the farm track. Thin plastic rippling and shimmering in the sunlight. The car came to a standstill several metres off the junction. The tyres ground against the rough terrain of the track, crunching on loose chippings and sparse gravel. Aran pushed open the door and stepped out into the crisp air. He looked confused, regarding the post box from a distance. He was sure that it had been broken, and he had left it lying in the verge. Yet here it stood as it always had, the same rusty forgotten colour. There was no hole in the side either.

The sound of the plastic bag billowing in the breeze was reminiscent of flying kites at the beach on a family holiday long since forgotten. Aran pulled down the red bag, examining the side of the post box. It had not been repaired; the metal here was pure and undamaged. Either he was going mad or someone was purposefully fooling with his mind.

It was then that he noticed the corner of an envelope poking out from the front of the post box. Pulling down the front lid, he withdrew the unsealed envelope. It was a note from Betty, the farmer's wife who was renting the cottage to him. It was nothing particularly important, merely apologising again that she had been unable to meet him on arrival or now when she was still busy. She reminded him that although he had preliminary booked the cottage for three months, if he wanted to quit earlier, he just had to let her know. She added the telephone number and address and said to call around if he needed anything. Or to pay the bill. There was always that mercenary element to any part of customer service. We want your money.

Under different circumstances Aran might have stayed longer. Despite the spartan conditions, he had been quite comfortable. All he had in his mind now was a desperate cry to flee this place before it permanently claimed his sanity. He would report Ludvine's murder. Call in on Betty, thank her for the help. Pay the bill. Leave. He glanced over his shoulder, back down the track. That horrendous graffiti was still smothering the cottage interior. He hoped it would wash off.

It was odd how relaxed he was feeling. Somehow, being out in daylight and away from the confines of the cottage calmed him. He was close to the open road, close to escape. He ought to have been more devastated, not only for the horrors that he had woken up to, but for Ludvine. He just felt numb, switched over to auto pilot to complete the necessities.

Flipping back the post box lid, he received a slight but sharp static electric shock from the hollow block of metal. Giving the post box a wary look but little more thought, he wandered back to his car, slinging the letter onto the passenger seat.

The drive to the village passed by without notice. Sensory functions seemed to shut down completely, relying fully on instinct and familiarity, the system of robotics that people with dull jobs use to avoid having to think about just how monotonous their existence is. Suddenly he was parked up in the village, the engine switched off, the keys still swinging in the ignition. It was time to report Ludvine's death, to accept it as reality. Say those words out loud. She has been murdered.

He was so lost in his thoughts that he did not watch his surroundings, and walked straight into the back of a stationary figure somewhere between himself and the telephone box.

Aran started his brief apology when the figure turned around and stared at him. He stopped. Quite literally.

Ludvine's expression crumpled to irritation when she discovered it was Aran Sellere. "I thought I asked you to leave me alone," she snapped, her manner immediately defensive.

Aran did not know how to respond. Ludvine was a corpse. She ought to be a ghost, having travelled up to heaven if such things really were true. No one simply got up and went home after having their intestines pulled out and their throat slit open. She was dead. He had seen her murdered. He had sat with her body that entire afternoon, unable to comprehend that she was actually dead. That she would never appear at the cottage. Never listen to her talk again. Never be able to wake in the morning and smell her hair, kiss her forehead, her lips…

"What is it this time?"

Ludvine's irritated demand interrupted his mystification. Aran blinked and looked her in the eye. She was real, a solid living being. She had never been killed. Yet she had. He had seen it. He had washed her blood from his hands when he had returned home. Both were facts, things that he had witnessed, had been able to reach out and touch. The two had to be true, and yet for one to exist, the other was impossible.

"Every time I have the misfortune of bumping into you, you accuse me of some rubbish. I'm mad, I have false teeth, I have serious memory loss… what will it be this time?"

Aran did not quite how to phrase what he was thinking. Perhaps it would have been better not to say anything at all but he could not stop himself. He was unaware of the reality, staring at her with wonderment and confusion. "But you're dead."

Ludvine narrowed her eyes. "What?"

"I saw him kill you."

Her face grew visibly paler. She took a step back as if he was carrying something contagious. A decision taken that he was mentally unstable. Perhaps also dangerous. In his odd little way, for no apparent reason, he was threatening her life. It was the first time anyone had ever hinted at killing her, and it was hard to know how to respond. The bright sunlight of the day was hardly the setting for hostile declarations, and the look on Aran's face was far from the ominous portent of death. "I don't know what your problem is," she started, taking a couple more steps away from him. "But if I so much as see you again, I am going to the police, do you understand me?"

"The police?" Aran did not understand. "But…"

"Stay away from me," she hissed defensively, darting out of the way as he moved towards her. "I know what you're up to. I suggest you get out of here and book yourself into a nut house."

Aran's hands dropped weakly as she hurried away. She had been genuinely scared of him. She had even been unaccustomed to the intimacy, looking horrified as he had moved as if to embrace her, to try and comfort her. He did not want to hurt her. Why would she think such a thing? Besides, she was dead. She wasn't supposed to be thinking anything. Except she was still alive. Maybe it was him and not Knight who had killed Ludvine. Ludvine who was still living, breathing, walking without a scratch. He understood nothing. This was insanity.

He was sure his fears were confirmed when he returned home to discover the writing on the walls, as the photographs, had completely vanished. If they had ever been there in the beginning.

Aran had collapsed onto the floor, his weight on the bruised shin that began to throb in pain again. At the very least the beating he had taken was real. Everything else was a confusion of perception. Perhaps he had dreamt everything. A waking dream of madness. The mad never notice they are mad, was that not a condition of pure insanity? He held his head in his hands, terrified of what lay beyond the cottage, but even more what lay within his own head. He seemed to have lost control completely. How do you catch the reigns of this uncontrollable psychological joyride? Rattling down the track with terrific speed, every stone felt with a vicious jolt. His tooth ached, or rather the space in his gums where the tooth had once been. He returned to that night when Staple had attacked him. The darkness crept up. Why had Staple attacked him? The man had been talking about Knight. Perhaps that had been wrong, only Aran's interpretation of events. Maybe Staple had been warning him away from Ludvine like a male beast defending his territory. The beating had been real. Yet it had seemed as real as Rachel Applegate walking in the garden, Ludvine pulling out her tooth, Knight murdering Ludvine, Ludvine's slashed body bleeding in the forest… images flashed through his mind, each as clear and real as the previous. This was not possible. There was no explanation. There was no way to know.

He was back in the lane, lying on the tarmac after Staple had finished kicking. Aran looked up and he saw the sign. Only pure desperation had tugged this irrelevant image out of his memory. He knew now that he had to go there, he had to try.

Pulling himself back onto his feet, he left the cottage.

The cottage lay just outside of the village. Creeping gingerly to the outskirts, knowing it did not belong, still craving contact. No interest was returned and the building was shunned. A squat little construction surrounded by a commotion of colour and shape, rich varied flowers, insects buzzing in the multitude. Ivy slowly trawled its way up the side of the front door, wishing to enter but not daring to cross the threshhold.

Aran stood on the rough track and stared up at the peaceful building. His eyes were fixed on that same brass plate that had caught his attention previously. The moment was imprinted, surrounded by darkness after Staple had left him bleeding on the damp and bloodied earth. 'The mathematician knows all'. A quick lesson in trigonometry really was the last thing he needed, and could serve no practical use, yet there was something reassuring in that short statement. It was something he had only now begun to appreciate. Previously he always had at least one person to understand, to talk to in the hope of being consoled. Now he was utterly isolated, sinking into his own miserable madness. This looked like the last stop before he hit the point of no return.

In all logical rationality he did not know why he was here. He would probably just stare at the cottage for a short while before leaving. The brass plaque looked like some kind of a joke. The sheen had worn off a long time ago. Mocking youth had died with time, and the owner could neither be bothered to keep the memento in good repair or simply take it down.

"If you're a salesman you'll have no luck here."

Normally Aran would have jumped at a voice so suddenly close behind. He merely turned around, apathetic.

An old woman waited, expectantly, in her seventies judging from her appearance. Her eyes wore the burden of heavy wrinkles as if she had spent her life laughing or reading complexly detailed books long into the night. Maybe both. Hanging off her saggy arm was a flat-bottomed garden basket filled with rich scented, delicately coloured wild flowers. There was a pair of glasses, complete with the long coloured string dangling around her neck, the glasses propped up in a nest of grey and white hair. A second pair were set upon her narrow nose.

The woman examined Aran with equal scrutiny. "You don't look much like a door-to-door though," she mused, squinting slightly to make certain what she thought was bruising on the side of his jaw was not just shadow. She wondered if he was the owner of the tooth she had found in her garden, but decided not to mention it unless he had come here specifically looking for it. Somehow there was a degree of embarrassment, either that or a convention about not mentioning discarded body parts. You were not supposed to pick up things that did not belong to you, and it was certainly verging on insanity to enquire to strangers if this tooth happened to have come from their mouth.

"I'm not," Aran assured her. "I was just…" He was not sure what he was or what he was doing anymore.

The woman raised her eyebrows encouragingly like a language teacher trying to tempt a few words out of an uncertain student. You can do it. Je. Suis… "You were just what?"

"I suppose I'm just passing through now," Aran looked dazed. Passing through but where was he going? He supposed he ought to try and find his way to the nearest psychiatrist's office. "I was working on a story here, but it fell through."

"Oh, a writer." The woman sounded politely interested. "Novels? Are you here to find a setting for your book?"

"I'm a journalist."

"Well, then, one can wonder why you are here. As far as the world of news is concerned, nothing ever happens here."

On the surface at least. The woman walked past him and up to the cottage, removing a key from her trouser pocket.

"Are you the mathematician?"

The key was in the lock, but not turned. The woman seemed frozen for a moment, almost shocked, before she looked back at him. "Yes, or at least I was." Her eyes glanced down to the side of the door, realising what had prompted his question. "Don't mind my silly little sign."

"It's your sign that brought me back here actually," he confessed.

The woman turned fully to look him straight in the eye. Perhaps he was the owner of the tooth. People, strangers, tourists, passers by, even the locals did not usually come this way, and certainly not more than once. But why should her sign be important to him? 'Oh' was all she said.

He could not stop himself. He had to explain to someone, anyone, before his brain burst. He needed someone to hear him, to tell him that he did really exist, that this moment was happening, not just a figment of his imagination. "I've been having an odd week, and for once in my life I honestly don't know how to explain it all away. I was here a couple of nights ago, I…" He faltered, not wanting to discuss the assault. "I saw your sign and I remembered it today. That the mathematician knows all. Not that you could. I don't suppose there is an explanation."

"But it can be good to talk," the old woman finished for him. She had a dull morning ahead of her own company until he had appeared, like a paper bag blown in. This kind of opportunity for company and conversation had to be grabbed. "And odd things do happen. Tell me, what is your name?"

"Aran Sellere."

She nodded as if it was to be expected. "Well, Aran, I am Maggie. Would you like to come in for a cup of tea? To be honest, you look as though you have a lot on your mind. It can sometimes help to talk things through, even if there are no answers to be gained. I don't get any visitors so it would be no trouble for me." She paused. "Another perspective on a problem can sometimes help loosen the knots."

His arrival at her cottage made little sense. The request for audience. The invitation into a stranger's house to talk of nothing. Nothing was part of the social norm. And what could he honestly expect to achieve? Nothing. He was reasonably convinced he was going mad. There was little this old woman could do to help except find medical help in the telephone directory.

In the kitchen Maggie busied herself with the kettle and the usual tea induced rigmarole: suitable cups from the cupboard, 'normal or fruit', 'milk and sugar' and so forth. Aran sat at the pine table, his hands held together as if he was about to confess to the mother superior. The sunlight from the window hit the side of his face with surprising strength. The brightened windowsill beside him was a jumbled clutter: pots of geraniums, forgotten birthday cards from years past. Caught in-between the plant pots, a standing thermometer, cookbooks and ornaments. Aran peered closely at a stone in the corner. It was a river-smoothed stone, a bluish grey mottled colour with the shape of a flattened egg. Someone had written the words 'one stone' on the surface in black paint. One single solitary stone lost in the chaos of the windowsill, which was probably reflective of Maggie's state of mind.

"Is that supposed to be ironic?"

"What?" Maggie glanced over as she set the sugar bowl and small glazed milk jug on the kitchen table. "Oh, you've found my home made art," she commented, realising he was referring to the stone. "You speak a bit of German, don't you?"

Aran was about to protest that it was written in English, but after a moment the connection clicked into place.

"I am a professor, would you believe it?" Maggie chuckled as she set a red teapot resembling a giant cherry on the table. "A professor of physics. Physics has been my life."

"And Einstein was a hero for you?"

"Well, I don't know whether hero is quite the right word. I suppose to a point one might say that," Maggie spoke as she sat down at the opposite side of the table. She placed two mugs down beside the teapot. "You see, when I was working at the university, I specialised in quantum physics..." she drifted off. "I don't know how much you know about these things."

"Very little," Aran admitted. "Science was never a subject that interested me at school."

"School." Maggie wrinkled her nose as if the very institution was an insult. A response to past memories or the basic nature of the learning process. "Life is very different from what we have drummed in to us at school. Anyway," she abruptly changed the subject, folding her hands neatly on top of one another. "What is it that has been troubling you?"

The amateur version of a visit to the psychiatrist. An alternative to anti depressant drugs that he probably should never have stopped taking. He opened his mouth to begin, not sure exactly how he ought to explain his circumstances, but stopped. "You are going to think I am crazy."

"I am probably mad too, so you are in good company," Maggie assured him good-naturedly. "So there's nothing to worry about. You just look like you need to get it all out of your system." She leant forward and began to pour the tea. "Well, you're not from this area, I've never seen you before. Why don't you start by telling me why you're here."

He parted his hands. He watched the steam twist up and out of the cup, the transparent wisps that looked like ghosts, something real and solid but actually little more than heat clashing against cooler air. The question was how to put these recent experiences into words. What to mention and what to retain. "I came here to work on a story," he started, looking up at her. "A story on Patrick Knight."

Maggie wrinkled her nose at the mere mention of the name. "The whole country has such admiration for the man," she muttered, although it was clear from the tone of her voice that she did not care to follow popular opinion.

Aran was mildly surprised by her reaction. He had never heard a member of the general public ever have a bad word to say about Patrick Knight. Here, the village was different from the rest of the country. Ludvine had never seemed very keen either. He let it go unquestioned. There was a sensation across his chest that made him feel that this was going to make him feel better.

"I was going to try and write about the real reasons for his sudden resignation. Try and find out. No one else had managed it but I had convinced myself I would succeed. I was going to write a biography. God only knows how…"

"And you didn't manage it?"

He wasn't sure how to respond. "I did and I didn't. I haven't got a story out. I don't suppose I ever will now. And I'm not even sure what the story is exactly if I were going to write it. But I've seen some strange things."

"Really?" Maggie looked curious. "What kind of strange things? Have you managed to get onto the estate?"

"Once. I told him I was writing a book about the local architectural history."

"I seem to remember I told him a similar line."

"Sorry?" Her unexpected statement threw him back out of their neutral territory. "But why would you need to get access to Knight under false pretences? I thought you said you were a physics professor…"

Maggie shook her head in a dismissive way. "Not important. Continue with your story. What strange things have you been seeing?"

"I saw a girl roaming his property. A girl who's been missing for a year." Aran said, guilt creeping up. The authorities still did not know. The teenagers had been forgotten, slowly fading from his memory just as they had from the interest of the media and the nation. The kicks from Staple had started the disintegration, but seeing Ludvine die had wiped away the last remnants. Nothing had seemed important now. "She was heavily pregnant. There's a body in the woods near his estate. It's been there for months. I can't help but think the two are connected. But I don't really know what's going on."

She had a look on her face that suggested these developments in the plot were little more than what could be expected. "I think he's responsible, yes. The Knights have always treated their women badly," she commented as she sipped at her hot tea. "But I haven't heard anything about this. Surely you would have gone to the papers or the police by now. Sitting on it like this, it's doing your career no good and it will only get you into trouble with the police."

"I did tell the police." Aran corrected her misconception. "I went to see the local constable, I told him everything, I gave him the picture I'd taken, the only evidence. I didn't know he was working for Knight. He attacked me the following night. I don't suppose anyone would believe me now."

"What about the body in the woods?"

"I haven't reported it. I... I got side tracked."

"How on earth would one come across a body in the woods? It must have just been dumped there to rot."

"Oh no, it had been buried. Someone I knew here showed me. I didn't manage to tell the police about it before... before everything happened."

"So these are the strange things that have been unsettling you?"

"No. However sordid it all is, it's all quite normal. It makes sense at least. It did make sense, I wasn't confused, but now…" He took a pause, running a hand through his hair. "Now I wonder if I've been under too much pressure recently. When I first came here, I met this girl, this woman. She lived in the village, worked as a cleaner here and there I think. She was so friendly, always interested. There was something about her, she was slightly eccentric, but it was so captivating." He broke off, catching a bleary look in Maggie's eyes. "Sorry, I'm rambling, missing the point."

"No you're not. What's her name?"

"Her name? It was Ludvine."

"It was Ludvine?" Maggie repeated. "Why are you referring to her as the past? Has she moved away?"

"No, she's still here. I think. I hope I have just confused dreams with reality. Although when I think back, there was always something odd about her. Sometimes when I met her, she had completely forgotten conversations we'd had, things we'd done. She would swear blind that we hadn't discussed this, hadn't been there, had never said that. I just thought she was teasing. She was always so convincing. And a couple of times she was suddenly so thin, I mean, painfully ill. She was just skin and bones quite literally. I wondered if she had a twin sister, but she was quite definite that she didn't have any siblings."

"Maybe this girl has some problems, mentally I mean."

"That was my theory too. The thing is, she was killed a couple of days ago. I saw it; up in the woods, Knight murdered her. He cut her throat, de boweled her… there was blood everywhere." It was painful talking about it. Like finally admitting to yourself that the affair was over. That you'd failed. She was dead. He would never see her again. "I stayed there with her all day. I remember it so clearly. The sounds, the taste of the air…" He lowered his head into his hands. "The thing is, she can't have been murdered…"

"But you just said you saw Knight kill her." Maggie was horrified. It was hard to imagine that such brutalities could take place in this idyllic rural setting. It did not seem possible that they could sit and discuss atrocities over the kitchen table like this.

"I know. But I saw her in the village the following day. She was alive and well. I spoke to her. I don't know what this is. Maybe she and Knight are trying to make me loose my mind, setting up murder, lying about a twin sister, trying to discredit my story with my insanity. Or maybe I am insane. My life has been shaken up and down quite a bit this year. Do you think strain can really do that to someone? Can it completely break down your comprehension of reality?"

Maggie gazed at his desperate eyes. He was pleading for an explanation, for the ending to come, swift and harsh if it had to be. He just wanted there to be a conclusion. She carefully set her cup onto the table.

"I think strain and stress can do a lot; play all kinds of tricks on one's mind. It may be as you say." She stopped, uncertain at first whether she should go on. She hadn't spoken to anyone about this for a long time. Her colleagues had laughed her out of the university. Here she was with a stranger. A man falling apart. "There may be another explanation," she started hesitantly. "There may well be a connection between Knight and this friend of yours, Ludvine, but not the one you would presume it to be. The Knight family seems to have been a draw for people coming to this village. It was the reason I moved here too. For my research. I read an old story, an anecdote I suppose you would say, about the Knights. A farmer, a tenant farmer had claimed to have met and spoken with one of Patrick Knight's ancestors' ghost, fifteen years after the man had passed away…"

"You're saying this has something to do with ghosts?" His tone was unimpressed. Immediately her credibility dropped into the lunatic fringe. She was not taking him seriously. He thought she had said she was a physics professor.

"No, I don't believe the man saw a ghost. I think he saw exactly who he said he saw."

"Fifteen years after his death?"

"Exactly. He saw a man, a solid, real living man who spoke to him. Although he knew he was dead. Does that sound familiar?"

Ludvine. The name was on his lips but he did not utter it. "You know as well as I do that's impossible."

She shook her head. "I don't mean to insult you, but you don't know what you're talking about. Theoretically it is possible. And it would seem that it has been proved to be possible. It's just not been documented scientifically yet. Although the case with your friend is far more complex, far more interesting, because you mention another version of her in very poor health."

"And you're going to tell me there's an explanation for that?"

"There's a theory." She leant back into her chair and considered him with interest. "Tell me, how much do you know about physics? Forget the basics they tell you at school. I mean real physics. Einstein's theory of elastic time for example. Or what do you know about quantum physics?"

"I'm sorry, I've never really had that much interest in science." Aran was lost. Caught out of his league, wondering where she was leading him. Perhaps she was just a lonely old woman who needed someone to talk to, maybe someone to teach as she sat and dreamed back to her old university days. Either way, it would be a distraction from his current troubles. He had been given his chance to talk, now it was her turn.

"I can explain what you need to understand." Maggie nodded to herself, seeing his bewilderment. "Time as you perceive it, does not exist."

"What?" Aran could not help but let the question escape as a scoffing laugh.

"Do you think time is actually moving now? Time is passing?"

"Well, of course it is."

"If you had studied physics, you wouldn't say that so easily as you do. The conception of time as we know of it in modern society is really a misconception, a myth. The rules of physics have shown this to be true. It is just that the difference between theory and what we observe in everyday life has not really been bridged. It makes this difficult for many to comprehend or accept."

It would have been easy to just call her a mad old bat and run away, shouting loudly enough to himself so that her words would be drowned out. But there was a keenness in the twinkle in her eyes that suggested she knew exactly what she was talking about.

"Of course time passes," he spoke. "I mean, it's always moving, we're not static. There's a past, there's a present, there's a future. It's ridiculous to state otherwise."

"It's ridiculous not to state it." Maggie retorted. "Tell me then, what is the past?"

"Something that has happened: me walking into your cottage for example."

"And the future?"

Aran smiled dryly. "I don't know what's in the future. It hasn't happened yet."

"But say, whatever will happen in five minutes time, you'd class that as the future."

"Sure."

"But in ten minutes time, that which you class as the future now, will be the past to you, following your logic. So events are never set in one particular position or another. Do you seen what I mean?" Maggie questioned earnestly. "The point from where you are observing is vital. In any experiment on any level, the mere observing of the experiment, the observer themselves will affect the results."

"You're just talking theory now, philosophy almost. Events still happen one after the other. In a chronological passing of time. Once something has happened, that's it, it's gone, it's the past. Time moves on."

"The concept of time movement is related to the idea of the speed of time. There are some miscomprehensions. This idea that time always moves at the same speed for example. That there is a universal moment. If I pressed pause at this very second, wherever you went in the world, in the galaxy, in the universe, everything would be paused at that same moment. It's nonsense, it doesn't exist. Even everything that you see at one second of a moment does not come from the same time as you."

Maggie pushed her cup and the teapot to the side of the table as she began her explanation. It had been some time since she had last taught, but she still had the gift for conveying information. "1905. Einstein's theory of elastic time. Time moves at different speeds. There is no universal moment. It all depends on your point of view, quite literally. The movement of time, as we perceive it, is relative to the speed of light. A day is the earth revolving once, us on the surface viewing it as the movement of the sun in the sky. We measure long distances in light years, don't we: the time it takes light to move from, oh, I don't know, say Jupiter to Earth. But if you go out tonight, not everything you see will be from the same time moment that you are experiencing. The stars that you see in the sky are actually in the past, as you consider it. You are seeing the past, for it takes years for the light from stars to reach the earth. Yet you say, the past is in the past, it has happened, it is done. You might think that it is lost to us. We see the past every night in the sky."

"All right." Aran relented slightly. "I follow what you're saying. The distance between the Earth and stars, well, it's massive, as you say. That's big scale. But what happens in our lives, here, it's small scale. You're just talking theory."

"You have to understand the theory before you put it into practice." Maggie calmly drummed her point into the table. "This is not just theory, it is practice on a grand scale. At the point of your observation at your moment, you see the past of the stars', thus there is no universal moment. Furthermore, the speed of time varies, depending on where you are. The further away from the earth's surface you are, the quicker time goes. This is an effect of gravity. The stronger the pull, the slower time goes. That's why a black hole is black. Black holes are collapsed stars; the gravity was that strong that the star collapsed in on itself. And because the gravity is that strong, time goes so slowly that it is frozen. The same goes for the speed of light in there. So slow, it doesn't move. There's no light, so it's black."

Aran slowly closed his eyes. "If you're trying to explain the presence of ghosts with this theory, I can't see how it works. It's too small scale. This explains nothing. You're dealing with astronomy, distances of millions and billions of miles. I am talking about one little village. That I saw Ludvine again…" He broke off, feeling his chest contract.

Maggie smiled sympathetically. "I am not trying to explain it with the theory of elastic time. I am just explaining this concept to you because it is important. I know, everyone is on the earth's surface, time moves the same for us all. But there are exceptions to the rule. Before I moved here, I specialised in quantum mechanics. It is far too complex to go into now and I haven't the energy to try and explain. A key issue in quantum mechanics is probability. We don't say yes or no, we say it's possible or improbable. Really everything is possible."

"You're telling me ghosts are possible?"

"I don't know about that." Maggie laughed. "I think most of that has been proved to be hyper sensitive attention seeking people but don't quote me. I don't think what you say, Ludvine, I don't think she was a ghost. She was real. She was living."

"But I saw her murdered!"

An awkward silence interrupted the discussion due to the intensity of Aran's protest. The words seemed to echo around the room, almost to an embarrassing level. So it was true, she really was dead. Maggie lowered her eyes, picking up a teaspoon. "If someone asked you if a person could walk through a wall, what would you say?"

Aran shrunk back into his chair, thankful she was not going to ask him to leave after his outburst. "Impossible."

"Exactly. But in quantum mechanics, we would say it is improbable. If you walked up to the wall now, you would certainly bump your head. But it is possible for materials to go through one another. There is a probability factor that it would happen, just as there is a probability factor that you would get heads if you flipped a coin. The problem is that the numbers you are dealing with for such a probability, for materials moving through one another, are so phenomenal, that it is mind boggling. For you to get that one in a something chance to walk through the wall, just as you need a one in two chance to get heads, you would have to keep walking up to that wall and bump your head constantly from now until eternity for it to work." She paused for breath. "But despite that, it is possible. Everything is possible.

"It is probable that dimensions exist, infinite dimensions, although to our perception, we will never know of them. These are, I believe, the infinite possibilities of the future. Every person is constantly making decisions that affect their future. Whether you came into this cottage to talk to me or not. There is another dimension existing in which you never spoke to me. Another one when you never came to this village. One where you did not go to the police with your discoveries, but went straight to the newspapers. They do not even have to be based on major decisions, it can be as simple as, do I throw this tea cup onto the floor or not? In turn, every one of these is related to every other choice and action of every other person. Other people's actions can affect your life as to whether a government declares war on another country, whether the bus drivers go on strike, whether that drunken man gets in his car that night or not. Everything is linked, creating even more possibilities, even more dimensions. They are quite literally infinite. There is an infinite number of Arans in other dimensions, living out every decision you did not take, making every mistake you did not make, every thing you wish you'd done. One of these will be so far flung from where you are and who you are, that he will be the anti Aran…" She paused, smiling to herself, a contagious reaction from Aran's own smile. "You've heard of antimatter. This relates to everything. And if you and the Anti Aran met, the reaction would be so powerful that existence as we know it would cease to exist. But this is just theory. How could we ever prove it?"

Aran sighed. "This is just academic discussion, something to do at university. It doesn't relate to real life."

"But it is real life," Maggie stressed the point earnestly. "Although everyday, in every action we are unaware of it. This is the problem, bridging the gap between what we call real life, and academic theory. This is what I had been researching for years. It's not as new as you might think. People have been aware of this phenomenon to some degree, for a long, long time.

"There is something special about this area. That's why I originally moved here, to try and study it on a more local level. For some reason there seems to be a rip in the continuum. Things slip through. Quantum mechanics can come into play, materials can move through one another. We can see flickers of other dimensions, the way life might have been."

"What exactly are you trying to say?"

"I think this girl you know, Ludvine… you've actually met more than one version of her. How many, I don't know. But I am enthralled that you have come into contact with this amazing phenomenon. All the years I have been here and I have never had any first hand experience to my knowledge."

"You're saying Ludvine doesn't really exist?"

"Of course she does." Maggie assured him. "What I mean is, that you've met more than one version of her. Ludvine when she decided to do this, Ludvine when she did not go there. The versions of her might not always be from the same time period as you either, considering the effects of time elasticity. I don't know how many you have come into contact with, only you have a chance of working that out."

"Just as which one is from my reality?"

"Exactly."

"But…" Aran stumbled for the right words. "Even if this were true, what's the point?"

"Does there have to be a point?" Maggie questioned. "All I know is that there is something special about this area. People have picked up on it for thousands of years. The megalithic societies were aware of it to some extent, as were the Celts, even if they didn't really comprehend what was happening. But because these civilisations did not leave any written records behind, we will never know now what they knew or believed. I have studied as much as I can from the local records. Information must have been lost, you can trace knowledge disappearing. In the Middle Ages they had a vague idea. Then nothing. Except for one family."

Maggie stopped for a moment, glancing across the kitchen as if half expecting to notice eavesdroppers. "I got access to the Knight family library several years ago. Whilst I was there I managed to read somethings I don't suppose Patrick Knight would have wanted me to read. The Knight to first come here, Charles Knight, a man with too much interest in the occult, knew about it." She stood up and walked over to a cupboard as she talked. "He wasn't stupid though, latched right onto what was happening. He knew exactly what he was doing when he built that house."

"How so?"

"Have you heard of ley lines?"

"Vaguely."

Maggie returned to the table, spreading a local map out like a tablecloth. "Monuments, important buildings are sometimes built upon what are called leylines. Basically they line up geographically. I am in two minds as to whether in most cases it means anything. However, take a look at the map. Here in the north we have a stone circle. Directly to the south of this, below the lake, is a barrow. There's a Celtic cross, here to the west. If you go to the east, you find the village church. I might add that the church is aligned perfectly, the spire heading off due east. The stone age, the Celts, the Middle Ages." She ticked them off on her fingers. "Now, if you drew lines here, north to south, east to west, what do you get at the intersection?"

Aran leaned forward, examining the map. "Knight's house."

"Exactly. It was built there for a reason."

"Are you saying Charles Knight was involved in the occult? He actually believed in these lines? I find it a bit hard to imagine Patrick Knight believing in something like that."

"Charles, Patrick, what's the difference." Maggie shrugged absently. "Have you ever been to the church? Seen the family graves, all lined up due east behind the church spire?"

Even Ludvine had mentioned the family graves. Several times. Several Ludvines, according to Maggie, anyway. Even the emaciated version of Ludvine. Which version was she? Which one could he actually consider to be 'his' Ludvine, the one that belonged to his own reality? How many had there been? Ludvine was dead. When he had seen her after the murder, she had returned to denial, fearful and forgetful of conversations. Conversations she had never partaken in. She had never lied to him, he realised, just as there never had been anything wrong with her mental constitution. He must have terrified her with his earnest talk of things he thought they had done. She did not belong to the dimension where Knight was completely insane and had butchered her. Aran would have to find her and apologise.

"Aran?"

He glanced up. The kitchen was silent.

"Have you been to the graveyard in the village?"

"Yes. They're all buried one after the other. But the fathers always died just after the birth of their sons."

Maggie smiled. "You noticed that too. I got into Knight's private library. Charles Knight was terrified of death. Well, I suppose he still is. He studied the occult. He learned about this practice of transference. The Knights have been practising it ever since. Women had been used as a mere commodity to their rituals. They have…"

"Wait," Aran interrupted. "What do you mean, Charles Knight is still afraid of death?"

"Patrick Knight, Charles Knight, they are essentially the same person."

"That's ridiculous."

"Improbable but possible. Material can move through material, remember?"

"But the graves in the churchyard," Aran protested. Someone had to keep her off the rails of academic theorising. "There will be a body for every headstone, we can go dig them up if you like. You can't fake something like what you're suggesting. Besides which, Patrick Knight was a child once, there's no question of that. There are school teachers who remember him, photographs…"

"It's a bit more complicated than that. I'm not talking about bodies. Of course every man died and was buried out in the church. A child was born. I'm talking about the transference of soul. Without a soul, the body dies. The same man has been hopping from one body to the next like a parasite. He learned the theory and found himself a place where the improbability of quantum physics could become possible, due to the rips in our dimension. There is a certain kind of energy here."

"You can't prove this."

"No, I can't. I'm too old now. But there is proof. You've seen the beginning of it. You saw the girl on his property. I don't suppose Patrick Knight has got long to live now." Maggie suddenly lurched forward, clasping his hands. "You have to try and stop it. Get the girl out of there. Physics has been my life, my passion, but I will never truly understand it, never be able to predict it and control it. That is to play God, don't you see? Knight has been playing God for too long. It has to stop."

"I don't know what you expect me to do." Aran pulled his hands away. For an old woman she was starting to become frightening. A little too intense in her conviction. "You can't just expect me to believe all this just like that."

"You know that she's there. Whether you want to call it playing God, dabbling in the occult or abduction and rape of a minor, call it what you will, but there are a million reasons why that girl should not be there. You're the only one who knows. You'll get no where with the police. You have to get her out of there yourself."

Aran stood up, now quite uncomfortable in the warm kitchen. She had been kind, calmly listening to his problems, helping him to clear his mind and offer explanations. Now he felt as though she was diseased, dangerous, something he had to flee from. Jumping to outlandish conclusions. "I don't know," he muttered.

"This has to end," Maggie called after him as he hurried to the front door. "Think of that girl. You can't let it happen again."

Maggie had gone senile in her old age. It was true that a lot of strange things had happened, and whilst Aran was now less convinced of his own dementia, he was not prepared to believe pure nonsense. Maggie's science explained everything neatly in theory, but how could he just accept her words as fact. Perhaps the physics was very valid – he wouldn't really know - but slot it into a real life context and it tasted wrong, out of place.

Relenting a little on final judgement, he decided she was right on one issue, that he would have to act alone to defend Rachel Applegate. Presently, he did not care for that sordid drama. He wanted to see Ludvine again, even if she would only scream and think him mad. He just needed to see her to know that she was real: neither a figment of his imagination nor the product of some complex blip in the regularity of physics.

It was already the middle of the afternoon. It did not feel as though he had been in Maggie's cottage that long. Two o'clock on a Tuesday. Ludvine took a class in the early afternoon so his best chance was to go to the community centre. If she was not already there, then she would soon arrive and in her own unique way be able to calm his fears.

Striding across the village green, Aran hurried towards the community centre. As he came around the corner, the building looked gloomy, almost in mourning for the loss of his mind. If that was the problem.

The windows were darkened. As though someone had been over the glass with a can of black spray paint. It was a little bewildering, but he did not immediately give it any attention. It was as if being blown forward by a gust of wind he stumbled up to the main doors. He pulled at the handle, but the doors merely jolted stubbornly, refusing to part. Aran blinked, for the first time properly examining the entrance. Someone had cleared the glass of the evening class signs, and had hammered roughly hewn pieces of plywood over the spaces where glass had originally slotted in.

Aran stepped apprehensively back from the building. Now that he thought about it, it really looked like a burnt out wreck, destroyed and discarded. It was waiting for someone to come and knock it down. It did not appear as though much had really been happening here for a long time. Yet he had seen Ludvine cleaning the centre only a couple of days ago. Surely he would have heard or noticed something if there had been a fire here in the past couple of days.

Puzzled, he wandered back towards the village green. He did not know what to do. He still did not know where Ludvine actually lived; the question of whether she was even still alive posing another complication. Maggie's theorising was preferable to his own madness, but it stood as a ridiculous defence against rumours of his own breakdown.

Adele Witherspoon, landlady to the Fox and Hound pub, was putting large umbrellas up on the wooden pub tables. Having set the final umbrella, this one advertising an Irish brand of stout, she looked up and immediately focused on Aran. "How's the work going?" She called over to him, blind to his bewildered wandering state as if he had just been hit by an articulated lorry. Somehow managing to walk away without any obvious inquiry.

He stopped close to the pub and peered over at her. Adele was real. This moment existed. It was absurd to suggest that any other moment, any other person could not be real. "I was just over at the community centre."

Adele wrinkled her nose. "It's a mess, isn't it?" she questioned rhetorically. "I wish they'd get on and do something about it, either knock it down or build it up…"

She spread out her hands as if mid debate. Her red painted fingernails reflected the sunlight. "But either way, do something. Just leaving it as it is does no one any favours. Of course, it's all a question of money, and no one wants to pay up."

"It was a fire that destroyed it?"

"Yeah, that's right. The building's pretty much gutted. It was a real wicked, nasty blaze."

"When did this happen? Was it last night?"

"Last night?" Adele burst out into laughter at the absurdity of the question. "You are joking, aren't you? That place was smouldering for days after. It must be six months at least since the fire."

"Six months?" Aran coughed up the time phrase like it had been blocking his throat. He had been here just over a week. When he had first entered the building, when he had first properly met Ludvine, it was certainly not the shell gutted by fire it was today. The room where Ludvine had danced alone looked as though it had been freshly painted. "But the evening classes," he started.

"Evening classes? They all finished with the fire."

The atmosphere grew slightly uncomfortable. Adele peered at him strangely as if he was mad, but was too polite to utter her suspicions out loud. "But there's nothing in the community centre, I promise you. That place is full of nothing but charcoal. Are you sure you're not thinking of something else?"

Aran shook his head. "I was there."

"But..." Adele faltered, not sure what to say. Normally she would have taken it good naturedly, as a joke intended to wind her up. But Aran was so earnest, so certain of what he was talking about. It was hard to find anything to smile about. "Are you sure you're all right?" she finally asked, giving him a concerned, mothering look. "It has been hot the past few days. If you don't drink enough you can suffer from heat exhaustion."

"I'm fine," Aran lied quickly. There was no point in continuing this conversation. The community centre had burned down. That was a fact to Adele, and clearly it was a fact for him. Whatever he had seen and experienced did not appear to exist anymore. "I'm just a bit tired. I've been to so many little villages that I must be getting them all muddled up."

The landlady seemed to relax, upon the surface at least. "That's probably it. You take care of yourself, now."

"I will." Aran said his goodbyes and hurried away, eager to return to his car. Ludvine seemed to be lost, and one way or another, Knight was to blame. He would return the favour in kind. It was time for Rachel Applegate to leave.

There was a strange, almost serene silence about the Knight mansion. The stonework literally glowed under the brilliant sunlight. It was virtually impossible to think that something so dark and cruel could ever have happened here. Dark histories lingered in every shadow cast, for nothing was pure anymore.

Aran approached from the east, entering by the gardens to the rear of the house. He crept like a ghost, his image filtering silently through the backdrop of shrubs and statues. Reaching the solid mansion wall, he pressed his back up against the brick work, closing his eyes. He was breathing heavily although he had not been running. Exhaustion did not usually come this quickly; it was the tension, the confusion in his head. Part of him did not care and was ready to walk away. But he forced himself to go through with this.

Catching his breath, straining with the slow twist, he peered in through the side of the window. The rows of books locked up within the library, never read by more than one set of eyes, considered him cautiously. There was no one in the library. The moment hung frozen in refined, intellectual thought. Time had stopped a long time ago. Perhaps Maggie was right. Time was an abstract; it would go at different speeds depending on the conditions.

Aran eventually circled the entire house, expecting to see someone through a window, hoping to hear a sound of life. There was nothing. The building looked like an empty museum. He returned to his starting point at the library windows, and began with the task of breaking and entering. His old battle wounds from the beating ached a signal warning reminding of what would come if he was caught.

The windows to this room were all locked, but they were in ill repair and this wasn't Aran's first break in.

Apprehensively he strode across the library, expecting to hear that cliché creak in the floorboards. The air was unearthly quiet. Somewhere a clock was beating, steady dull knocks of the pendulum swinging back and forth. The library door had been left open at a chink. Aran peered through the narrow space, to a Victorian corridor richly decorated, heavy in remembrance of an age long since past. It was liked stepping into a dream. The pure silence was surreal. He waited for Knight to come charging through, confident with the back up of Staple's brute force. Nothing happened. It was hard to believe that someone even lived here.

He followed the corridor's curve, halting at the cut off point of a closed door. Aran laid the palm of his hand against the wood as if checking for heat. He was really listening for any sound of someone on the other side, but there was no reading. He gingerly tried the door handle, his confidence growing as he felt that the door was unlocked.

A bright and unsurprisingly old-fashioned kitchen was revealed. The original tan red flag stones were still in place on the floor, as was the dominating range cut into the white wall to the right. There were three stone steps going from the doorway to ease the descent into the kitchen. Whilst technically still on the first floor, the habitual visitors of old, the staff, were certainly put in their place with this dug down room. These days, the era of solitude and the self inflicted isolation of Patrick Knight, there was no longer a staff at the mansion and most of the kitchen items and facilities here were little more than mementoes of times lost. Although the range had to still be in use considering the notable lack of a modern oven and hob top. The only surrender to modern times that he could see was the large fridge freezer humming in the far corner. Knight would obviously want to stock up on food. The less frequently he found it necessary to creep back out into society, the better.

Aran stood in front of the large kitchen table. Its surface was scratched and worn from decades of food preparation. It was still sturdy and solid, quite able to stand several decades more of labour. Carcasses would have been cut up here and prepared for roasting. Vegetables sliced, bread baked. It was all gone now.

There was a door in the far left-hand corner of the kitchen. It was a good inch lower than Aran's full height, and as he walked up to it, he noticed that it had not been closed properly. Touching the edge of the wooden door, he drew it open. Before him was a darkening passage of stone steps descending into the true belly of the mansion. Cold air greeted his face.

Aran squinted in concentration as a faded sound, created somewhere under the mansion, drifted up the passage. It was the cry of a woman in pain. He slipped into the passage, submerging himself into the subterranean pastures and heightening the sense of the sound. A woman was groaning in agony.

Aran slipped down the heavy stone staircase like black water. Downwards, arriving at a bare earthen passage covered over by medieval arches. There was an old, oppressive atmosphere, chilled frozen time. Everything seemed to have stopped. The air had a different taste, a finesse of age and of being forgotten. There were no lights on this level, leaving much of the surroundings a flat black shield concealing what he could only presume would be countless more vaults, corridors, cellars and rooms. The light from the kitchen followed him down the staircase, but when it reached the lower level it was too weak to reveal much. Aran shivered in realisation that literally anything could be positioned out there a few metres away from him. It was a black abyss, a black hole. You could theorise and work out the math, but the simple truth was that no one really knew what was there.

Another groan echoed down the corridor to his right. Darkness swelled up quickly, but a short distance beyond this a slit of warm, yellowed light cut through a chink in a doorway and laid a fan of illumination on the floor. The noise was coming from whatever lay beyond that door.

He was surprised to discover that he was as scared as he was. He had managed to break into Knight's property in a relative state of clear thinking. He had been drunk on apathy, had lost any deep feeling of connection with his own life. All he wanted he had lost and there was no real driving force left. Nothing but revenge. Now he was on edge, nervous and concerned over his survival again. He could actually hear the sound of his heart beating, noticeably faster than its usual lazy speed, ringing in his ears. His mouth was dry.

With stealth he took his attack to the lighted entrance. It was a heavy door, made of solid oak. The edges were worn and uneven now, he felt under his fingertips. He leaned up to the door and looked into the light.

Grime hung from the ceiling of a sorry looking vault. Bleak stone walls surrounded the cold grey flagstone floor. The air was cold and expectant, contained within. Dirty earthen floor. Markings that might have been circles, symbols, a ritual, but could just as easily be the remnants of scuffling footsteps. A tall black iron candlestick stood to the height of a lampshade beside a small lectern that had the unnerving resemblance of the predict that held the bible, almost like a pulpit. Wild fantasies of the occult and witchcraft, but the level was not connected with electricity and Knight simply had to revert to the methods of his ancestors. It was no more sinister than that.

In the centre of the room, on the ground, lay the figure of Rachel Applegate. She was on her back, enrobed in a long white shift that was probably too long for her if she had stood up and tried to walk. Escape did not appear to be an option she was actively considering at the moment. She lay, her large belly swelling upwards, and groaned. There was a film of sweat smoothed across her troubled face, and her eyes were scrunched, terrified in the knowledge that this was to be a natural birth. No painkillers, no help, no support. This was a return to the Middle Ages, a time when childbirth had been one of the biggest killers of women.

Patrick Knight was whispering rapidly to himself, fingers trawling over words in the book. It was hard to catch onto, maybe it was English, maybe it was something else. He looked desperate, having forgotten something or worried he would not finish in time. Not a man in control. In candle light, stood behind his lectern. He looked deranged.

Rachel Applegate cried out in pain. Whether Knight's books and memories held the secret to eternal life or not, Aran could not allow this experiment to continue. He was still hopefully unconvinced by Maggie's theorising. Pulling the door wide open, Aran marched into the cavern with a blank face.

Knight's words stuttered and fizzled out as the undetected intruder entered, hours from now when the birth was nigh. At this point Rachel was only in the very early stages of labour. Whatever he had been doing, the flow was now broken. He looked as though he didn't know what to do.

"You fool!" he suddenly burst out, the shock of such a passionate reaction catching even the girl's attention away from her private suffering. "Get out, or by god I will kill you."

Aran ignored him and crouched down beside Rachel. The girl stared desperately up at him, her eyes wide. She recognised him, the man who had visited the other week to view the architecture. He had offered her a way out, but she had been too scared to flee. She knew how desperate Knight was. A madman. Incoherent ramblings long into the night, slight recollections through drugged hazes that he had lived for hundreds of years. She had been a zombie for months, empty of hope. Resigned to the fact that she no longer lived, merely existed as a vessel for creating another life. A host to a parasite. Her senses had become dull over time with the torture, the repeated raping and the loss of contact with the rest of the world. Knight was cruel and domineering. She was still really only a little girl. He had soon broken her. After he had murdered Tanya, she had been alone. She had been certain she was mad. Yet now, suffering a new kind of pain, feeling the movement within her body, the sense of splitting, that she soon would be her own person again, the other life was strong enough to now exist on its own, she found herself caught up within a new clarity. She did not want this to happen.

Aran took her hand to show support. The girl stared desperately up at him, suddenly silent and bravely trying to master the pain.

"Can you walk?"

She nodded eagerly and slowly sat up, ignoring the protests that her body put out.

"Get away from her!" Knight came running at this. "Rachel, lie down or you know what will happen to you. Sellere, I should have asked Staple to finish you off. I didn't realise you would be this much trouble."

"The worst kind of trouble you could hope for." Aran told him. "You destroyed Ludvine. I destroy you."

Aran's odd comment stopped him, and he gasped on air. "Ludvine?" He did not understand.

"You murdered her." As he stared at Knight's face, he realised just how much he hated the man, how much he wanted to pummel his head against the stone floor until it was little more than bloodied pulp.

"But that was Tanya," Knight spoke without thinking. "I know no Ludvine."

He had confessed his crime as if it was a commonplace act. Rachel stood up on her feet. She wondered who Ludvine was. She would probably never know. Knight moved to drag her back like a tug o' war rope, but the stranger was fast, and pushed Knight away. Patrick stumbled backwards as if blown back by a hurricane. He slammed against the wall and his whole body seemed to implode, the air had been squeezed out of him. There was a sound of protest from his lips but the pain in his chest was too sharp. He collapsed to his knees.

"We've leaving." Aran took the shaking girl's hand and led her out of the room. They did not wait to see what Knight was doing, and did not dare look back. What exactly they feared was uncertain, whether it be a dying man desperate for aid, or a transformation into a demon. Anything seemed possible in the dark.

They hurried back along the corridor and up the stone steps into the kitchen. Bursting through the door, they entered the main hallway and fled towards the front entrance of the mansion. Drenched in sunlight as they staggered out onto the gravelled front of the old family estate. Aran could hear Rachel's heavy, pained breathing behind him, the weakening in her hand.

As they approached the main gates at the bottom of the drive, moving in a slow jog, he looked back at Rachel, shocked by how pale she was. "My car, it's a short distance from the gates. Do you want to wait here whilst I run on and get it. I'll go quicker…"

Rachel shook her head. "Don't leave me alone. He might come back." She paused, squeezing her eyes shut as another contraction tore through her frail body. "I can make it."

"All right." Aran relented. He looked back at the mansion. Knight had not followed them. Perhaps he had given up. It would have been easier to leave her here by the verge and sprint on ahead. He did not like forcing her to run down the road, bare foot at that. Yet after the past year, this ordeal probably paled in comparison, and was worth it for she was now free.

They followed the road instead of retracing Aran's route cross-country over fields. Regularly they would take a short pause as the agony became too much for Rachel to take. She would lean forward, breathing heavy short breaths and keeping her eyes shut as if not seeing would make it better.

A minute or so later, she would bravely raise her head, nod, and they would continue. Patrick Knight never tried to catch up.

There was an immense sense of relief as they finally saw his car parked up on the verge. Rachel said that she wanted to lie down, so he opened up the back seat door and let her clamber in. It would be the most space she would have to stretch out until they arrived at the hospital. He had wondered about calling an ambulance as they had hurried to his car, but it would take time for an ambulance to get to this far-flung corner of the countryside. It would be quicker for him to drive her out to the nearest town to get medical attention.

They talked during the long journey. If it could be called talking. Rachel's constitution, both physically and mentally was long past normality; Aran's mind was balanced against insanity. Bland, comforting conversation avoiding the obvious subjects. Pretending it was all right. Talk of films and music, all at least a year old. Caught in another strange time limbo.

Rachel's voice was drawn from a pit of pain; her words cut up as she tried to keep calm, praying that they would make it to the hospital before she gave birth. She did not know much about this natural process, pictures from biology textbooks vaguely remembered, educational videos the class had endured, embarrassed by the details, disconnected from the reality. They considered it as something that old women experienced (and by old women she meant adults, anything from twenty to forty). In their adulthood and wisdom they would know the facts, the signs and what to do. They would cope. Rachel knew that her water had broken. That one had been hard to miss. She knew she was experiencing contractions, although she had never thought to try and time the space between each one, and she had no idea how far on she was. Even though she was now giving birth, the thought was still alien to her. She did not know what to do with a baby. She hoped they would not expect her to keep it.

Aran broke the speed limit repeatedly. Signposted warnings of speed cameras proved to be lies. Thankfully police cars were elsewhere that afternoon. If he had been pulled over for speeding, when they had seen who was in the back seat, they would hopefully have encouraged him to continue, maybe even given him a police escort. Aran indulged himself in this little heroic fantasy as he followed the confusing inner city signs that led him out to the hospital.

He drove like a lunatic through the hospital grounds, bumping up and over curbs, leaving tyre ruts through flower beds. Off-pink signs like markers for tourist attractions lead the way through the maze to the maternity wing. The car skidded to a halt in a small parking area around the back of a sterile looking building. A man was pushing his pregnant spouse in a wheelchair up a ramp into the entrance. Further away from the door a skinny woman with lank brown hair stood and moodily sucked on a lit cigarette.

"We're here!" he declared triumphantly, twisting against the seat belt, expecting to see her eternally grateful face gleaming back at him. All that he saw was a small ragged cardboard box full of paperback books on the back seat. Rachel Applegate was not there.

"Shit," he cursed, his first thought being that she had somehow tumbled out without him noticing. He stared at the box. No one had been lying in the back of his car recently. He wondered if she ever even existed. This could not be right. He had talked with her, seen her reflection in the windscreen mirror. At what point had she simply disappeared, ceased to exist?

He jumped as someone tapped on the side window. He was met with the irritated face of a nurse. Aran wound down the window.

"You can't park here," she snapped. "The ambulances need to be able to get through."

Aran stared dumbly up at her as if she was speaking a foreign language. "Oh, I'm sorry," he finally spoke, starting the ignition. "I'll get out of your way."

Leaving the window down to feel the reassuring brush of the breeze against his face, he drove out of the hospital grounds. He wondered if in another reality somewhere, he had managed to deliver Rachel to the hospital in time. He wondered if it had been a boy or a girl.

A newspaper lay on the kitchen table. The front-page lay facing down against the grain of the wood. The print was hidden. Those shocking headlines in the minds of the country, on the lips of many - Patrick Knight was dead. His body had been discovered in the family home yesterday sometime during the afternoon. One of the major supermarket chains had been delivering a large supply of groceries that Knight had ordered a couple of days prior. He had been uncompromising on which day they could deliver. The date and time had been designated, as he was certain to be home then. It seemed a little unhelpful considering his reputation for never leaving the manor grounds.

When the delivery man had arrived, the building had been oddly silent. He had not really thought about it until retrospect hit, he had told baying reporters. He hadn't thought as he'd driven up through the gateway, left half open as if broken. He had knocked on the door and called the telephone number without any reaction. He needed a signature and he still had two other deliveries to make. Loitering outside in the intense summer heat, he had gazed up at the sprawling self-indulgent might of the building and guessed that the man who lived here simply had not heard. He had tried the door, discovered it open and entered.

He had discovered Patrick Knight on his face in the library, clutching an old hand-written family tome. The man was dead, not only that but cold. After the obligatory autopsy, it was declared that the retired politician had died of a fatal heart attack, a death completely without suspicion as had first been the presumption. Everyone wanted a conspiracy, but there was nothing dramatic to be pried out of the facts. Apparently a weak heart had plagued the Knight family for generations. Most of the Knight men had never made it far beyond fifty. Patrick had proved to be no exception. He would be the last in the chain. Maybe that was why he had never married. Or maybe not.

Following the reckoning provided by the autopsy, by the time the delivery man entered the mansion, Patrick Knight had already been dead for over twenty-four hours. That was the penalty of living alone. No one noticed when you stopped existing.

Aran had worked out the simple maths to the conclusion that Knight had died a couple of hours before he had broken into the building and rescued Rachel Applegate. He knew that should be impossible. He had seen them. Yet Rachel had not been in his car when he had arrived ungraciously at the hospital. Knight was dead by that afternoon. He had not been down in the cellar. Nothing had happened as he remembered. Yet if it was all a lie, what had he, Aran, been doing during those hours? Driving wildly through the countryside following hallucinations? Even if he had been caught up in a parallel dimension, surely he had still broken into the house. Why had he not seen the body in the library? Or maybe he had gone to another dimension. But then what of his reality? Had he just disappeared from existence for those precious hours? Maggie's nonsense was infiltrating his brain; he was daring to believe. His logic called him a fool. He was breaking up.

Somewhere in the middle of irrelevancies and small articles few ever bothered to take in, was a short piece. It concerned a case that had hit the nationals over a year ago, but as the weeks had drawn on and no conclusion was reached, people had grown bored and stopped caring. Now they knew what had happened, but it was too late to ever make a noticeable mark on the national consciousness. Tanya Cole and Rachel Applegate had been found in Liverpool. Alive but not well. Rachel Applegate was several months pregnant and Tanya was HIV positive. Both girls had been completely unaware of where they were, drug addled and traumatised, when the Salvation Army woman had found them sitting in the gutter, giggling like loons. The authorities were still not really sure what had happened to those missing months, or even how the abduction, if it had been an abduction, had been conducted. Until the last of the drugs left the girl's systems, they would not get any sense out of them. Even then, no one could really be sure how much the girls would be able to remember. A year had just disappeared.

Aran felt a fool on so many levels. Although he had never tried to get anything published, which he considered one of his few remaining blessings, it was as though the last of his journalistic integrity had been flushed down the toilet. As far as he was aware, he could have arrived at this village and merely lain in the cottage in a madness-induced daze for the past week for all the real things he had actually experienced. And now it was time to leave.

He had contacted his landlady, Betty, yesterday and informed her that he wished to leave. He had paid the bill – a full month even though he had not stayed that long. In the cottage he had almost completed packing his belongings back into the boxes and bags. He had not yet started the dubious and stressful task of fixing everything back into his car. It was a certain fact that it would all fit in the vehicle, because it had all been crammed within the metal confinement upon arrival. It was a complex three-dimensional puzzle. There was only one pattern that would fit and Aran could not recall exactly which box it was that he should start with. He would drive into the village to pick up a few supplies for the journey first, then come back and pack, telling himself that it was the most sensible approach and not that he was merely avoiding that which had to be done.

Light chalky dust from the grinding tyres drifted up into the hot air as the car bumped its way up the farm track towards the main road. The heat shimmered lazily in the surrounding fields. The intense blue sky stretched out across the atmosphere above. Ahead in the middle of the road where the track drew up to the relative comfort of a tarmac surface, lay a shiny green object.

Aran brought the car to a standstill and pulled on the hand brake. Without bothering to switch off the engine, he removed himself from the vehicle and stalked out to the foreign object. Crouching down, he picked it up and turned it over in his hands. It was some kind of paperweight, about the size of a large man's fist. A smooth half bubble of moss green glass, with a little scene of a small thatched cottage floating within the transparent material. Aran glowered down at the cottage caught up in its idyllic hopes, protected by the thick glass surround. If that cottage were introduced to real life it would be a ruin within ten years. Weather damage and age would eat away at the walls. The occupants would argue and leave each other. Either that or they would simply disappear. As if they had never existed at all.

His fingers tightened furiously around the cool glass tear, anger and frustration growing. He did not want to be reminded of what he almost had. He lobbed the paperweight away into the fields, venting his anger on inanimate objects, for there was nothing remaining for him to blame. His aim had not been high and the paperweight hit the post box standing by the fence. There was a loud bang as the glass object ripped a hole through the rusting metal shell. Unbalanced by the sudden attack, the post box dropped to the ground, either diving for cover or exhaustedly admitting defeat and giving up.

He watched as the post box fell, the dust lurching up on rebound. The sound of the paperweight landing somewhere in the grass cut like a dull thud. Then silence returned. Everything was still again.

He stared at the post box. He had seen this before. Not the destruction, which had been mindless and unintentional on his part, but the result, the broken mail box. He had found it in the road in this manner the day he was sure he had gone insane. He had picked it up and tossed it into the verge, as he now found himself doing again. This time the post box truly was damaged, in his own version of existence. What was it he had seen the first time? A future echo of what his anger and frustration would produce? Whatever it was, it did not serve any purpose as far as Aran could infer. He had not intended to destroy the post box and it was too late for regret now.

Getting into his car, he slammed the door shut and drove away to the village.

It was the village fete. Aran had forgotten, and stepping from his car, he began to feel nauseous. Surrounded by this summer bubble of happiness. The glaring reality of everything else was getting to be too much. Imprisoned in a giant glass paperweight complete with twee chocolate box scene, so idyllic and simplistic that it was hard to breathe. He did not want to see their smiles, people dancing, children laughing, the air drunk with the sensation of being care free. How could they be like this after everything that had happened? They didn't understand suffering the like of which he had endured. If any of his experiences had ever really existed at all. At the peak of confusion now, with no idea what could be relied upon. Up there he knew he could never come back down without falling into insanity. He would have to try and learn to live with his knowledge and his experiences. If that was possible.

Hung over, having to face the morning after, surrounded by smug sober people. Aran carefully sauntered in the direction of the village shop. He skirted around groups of locals, avoiding eye contact, wishing he had thought to bring his sunglasses with him. Colours of streamers, banners and balloons illuminated by the sunlight bit into the back of his retinas.

"You still here? I heard you were leaving town."

Aran took a shocked step backwards as a white-faced clown with green curly hair and black line eyebrows drawn onto his forehead suddenly shoved his face without apology in Aran's path.

"Not that we're trying to get rid of you," the clown added in a friendly tone. "Visitors are all welcome. Betty just mentioned that you were moving on. End of the holiday I suppose."

He stared blankly back at the baggy-suited man. Who the hell was he? It was hard to draw a line of recognition when faced with a man in too much face paint, a bad wig and shoes at least twice the size of his actual feet. Yet the voice was familiar, and under normal, more favourable circumstances Aran would have quickly placed it. Today he was too worn out to function at a regular pace.

The clown's oversized silly red mouth broke out into a wide smile. "You don't recognise me, do you? I must say I'm rather grateful. Dressed up like a right dog's dinner. I didn't want to do it, but Adele kept on at me, 'it's for a good cause.'" He pulled a grimace of an expression as he mimicked Adele's voice.

"Bill?" Aran's eyes widened as he finally realised who he was talking to. The landlord of the Fox and Hound. Of course, now that he plugged back into his brain, switching on his memories, he could recall something about Bill as a clown. Ludvine had been chattering about it once, that she had seen Bill dressed like this. That must have been last year. From what she had said, he had been just as disgruntled then. How had they persuaded him into a repeat performance?

"You do well to look horrified," Bill advised. "But not as horrified as myself. I can not believe I agreed to do this. Never again, I will promise you that."

"What? Twice is enough for any man?"

Bill chuckled at the thought, his surface amusement covering a genuine shudder. "Don't give me nightmares, now. No, this is the first and last time I will be partaking in such things."

Aran's brow wrinkled in confusion. "But Ludvine said…"

"Ludvine?" Bill interrupted, cutting off Aran's chance to show his presumed insanity. "Well I never, it is a small world. How do you know Ludvine then? I haven't seen her for a good few years now."

Aran opened his mouth to say something, then stopped. He was lost, utterly lost in the moment. Overwhelmed by contradictory facts. What he should say to this man so as to not cause alarm? This was all wrong. Ludvine had told him that she had seen Bill dressed as a clown a year ago. Why would she lie? Or why would Bill lie for that matter? Recent events had proved Ludvine to be a non-entity, a thing that did not exist. Bill knew her. She had not been here for several years. Ludvine had mentioned living in Denmark before returning home to the bewildering sight of Bill dressed as a clown. Somehow he must have skipped ahead to the future without realising it.

"I met her when I was over in Copenhagen," he lied dumbly to Bill.

The man accepted the statement without question. "Yeah, she moved over to Denmark a couple of years ago. Best thing really, there was nothing for her here. Was she doing all right when you saw her?"

"Yeah, fine. Working as a translator if I remember rightly."

Bill nodded as if he was the proud father. "Glad to hear it."

There was a sudden jolt within his body, a mental plead begging him to run away. "Listen Bill, I've got to go, haven't got much time."

"Of course, life of the journalist." Bill nodded as if he understood. "Safe journey."

"Yeah, thanks," Aran murmured numbly as he walked away. This short visit had truly been life changing. He had somehow witnessed future echoes. Ludvine had told him of this moment, this insignificant day when Bill would dress as a clown. Just as he had already seen the destruction of the post box. The hole bashed in the side of the rusting metal casing. The entire piece lying in the dust in the road. The first time he had seen it had been that same day when his world had been crushed permanently. The day Knight had butchered Ludvine out in the woods. A murder born of insanity, committed without reason.

Aran stopped across the road from a public footpath sign. He had followed that footpath on the day when he had witnessed her murder. The day he had been too useless to save her from that monster. The day that had started with a future echo.

He looked back over his shoulder to gaze down the road. Bill was stood with three green balloons in one hand, leaning forward as he talked to two small children. This was a messed up place. There probably was no meaning to the blips in the continuation of reality. Probably. But everything was possible, even if the chance was so small it was virtually impossible. That was something Maggie had taught him.

Aran started to run. His mind tumbled over itself. He ran up the narrow footpath, tearing free from the village and into the open countryside. He rushed through fields, the breeze whipping against his face, the blades of grass almost clawing against his boots. In his eagerness to get to the woods, he almost fell down onto his face as he tried to clamber over a style quicker than was humanly possible. Approaching the forest, he saw everything was just as he remembered. Even the girl walking up into the trees.

Ludvine.

He would have stopped to shout out her name, wave frantically to try and catch her attention. He did neither and continued running. He did not want the horror to repeat. He had to stop it.

Reaching the tree line, he realised this wasn't happening as he remembered. The first time he had seen Knight enter the forest after Ludvine. He had seen the second figure. There was only Ludvine today. If Aran had been thinking rationally, he would also have reminded himself that Knight could not go out walking as he had recently died of a heart attack. On a more worrying level, the second figure following Ludvine into the forest was Aran Sellere. No, he would never do anything like that to her. He had been given a second chance. He was overjoyed to realise that she did exist. No one would take that away from him.

The cooling shadows of the trees clashed against the hot humid air of the summer. Insects buzzed at his ears. He pushed away branches and undergrowth, desperate to locate her but horrified to find that she had disappeared from sight.

Aran slowed down, the sound of his heart beating, a pained repetitive scream in his ears. He was moving too fast to think clearly. What should he do now? The forest was spinning around him. Everywhere he looked he was greeted with the same view of cluttered disorganised trees, lit up by sunlight breaking through between the complex network of leaves over head.

Movement up ahead caught his attention and he followed it. The air stuck in his throat as he saw Ludvine in the distance. She was alive, just as he remembered. The sunlight flowed down her loose hair. Her eyes were outlined in black. She moved silently, as if in a dream, settling back into old routes and haunts as she returned home. She stepped up to a moss covered rock, and swung herself around to perch upon it as if she were an imp. Leaning back against a tree trunk, she wrapped her arms around her huddled legs and gazed blissfully up at the ceiling of foliage.

"Excuse me, are you Ludvine?"

The peace was festering. She did not know yet. She was innocent of the corruption, of the hate, of the brutality. Her attention shifted to someone close by whom Aran could not see. He started to run. Ludvine did not notice. She looked across at the man who had just spoken, a little taken aback that he knew who she was. "Yes, why?"

"I've been looking for you."

Her eyelids stretched wide apart as she saw him reveal the hunting knife. "What the hell?" she shouted out as he lunged out to stab her. She stumbled back off her rock.

Numbness flooding her nervous system. Breathing heavily, her chest tightening as if someone had set a lead weight upon her ribcage. People were always warned not to go out on their own, not to disappear. There were lunatics everywhere. She had just never thought that she would meet one out here.

Knight snatched at her arm as she tried to run away, swinging at her with his knife. He was full of rage, furious that his life had been cut short. He was supposed to have been immortal. She was completely disconnected to his torment, but she was the perfect and obvious person to vent his woe on. A name mentioned in a dark, dank cellar.

"No!" Ludvine broke out, her voice somewhere between a scream and a sob. She kicked out at him without thinking, automatic self-defence mechanism.

Knight winced but did not release her arm.

Without obvious reason or logic a third figure appeared, running into the side of Knight and aggressively pushing him away. Ludvine had always presumed the forests to be empty. People generally didn't like to walk far these days. If she had known that there were so many solitary men roaming she would never have come. Things had certainly changed in the few years she had been away. She stumbled backwards as Knight's fingers unwillingly released her arm. Unprepared for the jolt, she tripped up on a tree root.

Aran swung around at Knight, punching him in the side of the face. He was too determined to stop the course of events to even question how a supposedly dead man could be out in the woods threatening young women with knives.

"Will you never disappear?" Knight howled, grabbing Aran roughly by the shoulder and stabbing towards him with the knife. One failed attempt, then his arms crumpled as he was hit in the stomach with a broken log. His body seemed to fold up around the uneven surface of the branch as if admitting defeat. He dropped the knife.

Aran was just as surprised as Knight, and looked around to see Ludvine as she pulled the branch away from Knight.

She gripped her weapon with both hands, her eyes wild as she prepared for a counter attack.

Like a deflating balloon, Knight changed, becoming the ageing man that he was. The air wheezed out of his body, almost a chore to remember to breathe regularly. His face collapsed. Everything was lost now. This was the end.

"What the hell do you think you're doing?" Aran yelled at him.

Knight did not look him in the eye. "You took my future away," he spoke, lamenting the loss of Rachel and the baby. Those last few moments would haunt him until he died. This time something had gone wrong. He did not understand. And the angry accusations about a woman called Ludvine. He had never even met such a person. The following days as his anger and his bitterness swelled, he knew what he would do.

Aran kicked the man away. There did not seem to be much else to do. Knight had lost his knife. No longer a worthy predator. He was a pathetic sight. He could not return intention with intention and kill Knight. The man was not worth such a dramatic end. "Get the fuck out of here."

Knight complied without question.

His ribs swelled out as the air rushed down to his lungs. Cold sweat of fear settled on his back. Aran slowly turned to see if Ludvine was still there. She had not disappeared, this time she did exist. There were no signs, no pointers to denote authenticity, but he knew that she was from his own reality. She was not dead. She was his Ludvine.

Her brave front crumpled as Knight departed and the branch she had lofted fell uselessly from her fingers. Distress crossed her face and Ludvine ran shaking fingers through her hair. "What the hell just happened there?"

"Just some nut, it's over now," Aran assured her.

"You hear about these things happening." Ludvine continued, not really talking to him, just babbling, trying to keep a grasp on her sanity, on her nerve. Inside she felt as though she was about to collapse. "Roaming lunatics. You just never think that it will happen to you. I didn't know what to do when he took out that knife."

She accepted his arms without question as he stepped up to her, allowing him to embrace her. He could be just as homicidal as the other one, but the possibility did not occur to her. "And the stupid thing was, all I could think was that he looked just like that MP, you know, Patrick Knight. But he's dead; he died a couple of days ago. It was in all the papers at the airport."

"Just a coincidence." He was surprised by how calm he was. "I think we should get back to the village, just in case he decides to come back."

Ludvine nodded numbly, stepping back from him. "You're right." She paused, looking him in the eye without any recognition. "Thank you. I don't think I can ever say that enough. I doubt I could have handled him on my own. Thank you, whoever you are."

He realised that she was not his Ludvine. They had never met. This was the first moment. Everything he had experienced with her before this point had been a lie, a figment of the imagination, a cruel prank of the fickle nature of physics if Maggie had her way. His Ludvine did not exist. She was not even Ludvine. For this girl who stood before him now was the true Ludvine. They were strangers. Intimacy gone.

"No problem." He smiled weakly. "I'm sure you'd have done the same for me."

Aran woke up the next day sprawled out on his back. Staring at the living room ceiling. He was alone. Slowly, he forced himself up into a seated position, wincing at the aches in his back. Why had he slept down here when there was a bed upstairs? He could not remember much of yesterday. His eyes settled on a half empty bottle and the basic details groggily trudged back into his memory. He had returned to the village with Ludvine. They had soon parted. He had driven home and consoled himself with whisky. He had never had much of a head for hard spirits and guessed that he must have passed out sometime during the afternoon.

The poor pitiful lunatic discovering that Ludvine had never existed. The tragic lover when he had witnessed her murder, unable to save her. Someone else he didn't know was still alive. It all boiled up to a great deal of sympathy and self pity, all combined could have justifiably seen him through the rest of his life as a miserable recluse. Now there was nothing. His career was dead. His meaning was lost. He had been emptied. He had lost the love of his life, the spark that had made him feel like he wanted to try again. Even then, life had not been satisfied, and had chosen to wave her temptingly in his face. Yes, actually she is real, but she is a stranger to you. Ha ha.

He had no more energy. He resigned himself to existing robotically, to lead a mediocre life. He did not know what he would do; all he had decided was that he was leaving as soon as he had packed.

Wandering through to the kitchen, the whisky bottle dangling loosely in his fingers. He silently watched as he poured the rest of the alcohol down the drain, not sure why he was doing it, but convinced that the answer, whatever it might be, did not lie in the bottle.

He spent the next hour packing up his possessions into his overworked, exhausted car. He did not really think about what he was doing, and unintentionally it worked, the boxes automatically slotting back into place. The magic puzzle was solved. His car was tightly filled with books, camera equipment, kitchen utensils, clothes, bedding and other random items – the remnants of a life. The cottage was empty and void of character again. It was as if he had never been there.

Lazily swinging the passenger side door shut, he stalked back into the cottage to make one final check. He had not forgotten anything. The rooms were bare and sad, waiting to be completed. Maybe one day Betty would finish renovating this place.

His footsteps thumped down the staircase. This was it, the end, time to go. He still could not quite believe that everything that had happened really had occurred. He hoped or expected he would wake up. Ludvine would assure him it was just a dream. But when he slapped himself in the face he recognised the sting. This was reality.

Locking the French windows, Aran turned to face his car. Propped up against the passenger side was a large dark blue hard core hiker's rucksack. It was so tightly and expertly packed that it looked as though the slightest move would burst it. Aran squinted at the item in confusion. He would have merely presumed he had forgotten to pack something except that it was not his rucksack.

"Sorry I'm a bit late."

He visibly jumped at the sound of a voice from behind. Turning, he discovered Ludvine leant up against the cottage wall. She considered him intently, her eyes steady, and as always dark rimmed.

"Ludvine," he started in confusion, really not sure what to say to her. "Are you all right, after yesterday?"

"I suppose so," she sighed, shrugging her shoulders. "I didn't sleep well last night, I must admit. I finally got off to sleep then it was time to get up." She paused awkwardly, as if worried something had changed over night. "So, are we off then?"

"We?" Aran repeated, wondering if it was just a figure of speech.

"Yes, like we agreed last night!" Ludvine laughed. "Don't tell me you've forgotten. You can't do that. I can't get stuck here again, especially after what happened yesterday. I don't really belong here anymore. I need to start over again. You said you're off up to Scotland. I'm going with you, remember?"

There was a delay in working the information through his mind. They had never had that conversation. "What are you talking about?"

A touch of uncertainty hit her face. "You are winding me up now, right? We talked all day yesterday, all evening as well as I remember. We said we'd get away from this place," she paused, biting her bottom lip. Perhaps he had just been joking. Drunken merriment with a stranger. "Have you changed your mind?"

This had never happened, at least not to him. In this reality they were still strangers, yet whilst they stayed in this village, they seemed to be getting to know one another without ever having to meet. To get to know the real Ludvine, they would have to go away. He nodded, slowly at first, but more confidently as he realised what had happened and what he should do. "I'm just winding you up. Of course I haven't changed my mind."

Ludvine breathed a visible sigh of relief. "Thank God for that. I thought we'd been getting on well last night and I wondered for a second there it had all been an act."

Aran gazed over at her. He wished he had been there. "Is this all you've got?"

She laughed. "Are you joking? With my music obsession? No, these are just the essentials. I asked Adele to send up the rest to me when I've got an address. You said your car was pretty packed so I thought the CD collection could wait for now."

"I wasn't joking about the car at least, but I think I can squeeze this in the back seat." Aran picked up the rucksack. Ludvine scampered across as he opened the back door. Unzipping one of the side pockets, she pulled out a CD case and broke out into a grin. "Well, I only brought the one. We have to have something to listen to in the car, right?"

Aran smiled back at her. There was something there that had been missing yesterday. The one thing that the old Ludvine had. Recognition. It was starting to grow in her eyes. This was the beginning. Pushing her rucksack into the back of his groaning car, he slammed the door shut and sauntered around to the driver's side. Life was very strange. But it was getting better.

Ludvine switched on the CD player as Aran turned the keys in the ignition. Removing the shimmering disk, colours of the rainbow reflected from nowhere, light was sliced up into its various possibilities, she put the music into the machine.

Aran looked over at Ludvine as she settled herself into the seat the same way she had last time. As she met his eye, realising she was being watched, he gave her an incredulous look. "Is this the latest music for your repertoire of alternative belly dancing?"

Ludvine was a frozen image of herself. She stared at her new companion, trying to penetrate his thoughts without success. "How in hell's name do you know about that?"

Aran grinned slyly, slinging an arm around the passenger seat. Watching through what visibility was left in the back window, he reversed the car.

"Well?" Ludvine demanded as he swung the car around to face the track up to the main road.

Aran shrugged. "Just a lucky guess."

Somewhere else Aran woke up suddenly as if someone had cruelly just screamed in his ear. Gasping for air, he lowered his head to its original position, surprised to feel the hard solid touch of the floor against the back of his skull. The living room ceiling hung overhead. He must have fallen asleep on the floor.

A throbbing in his temples began to build. A distant hum, somewhere miles away someone pounded a drum. He abruptly sat up, squeezing his eyes shut as a sensation of dizziness swept over.

Gradually, he opened his eyes and dared to peer across the room. The ache in his head made him acutely aware of every sound and movement. Everything seemed to be as he remembered, except for the half empty bottle of whiskey just out of arm's length. That had been full, the last he remembered. He must have been consoling himself with alcohol, although he could not really remember why. Ludvine was involved somehow, even though she was gone now. He had saved her, but the girl he had saved... he closed his eyes as he slowly began to remember. She was not the same person he had first met.

Robotically, with stiff limbs, he dragged himself up and surveyed the spread of packed boxes and bags waiting to be placed in the boot of his car. His lease at the cottage had ended and it was time to move on. He did not know where he was going but he had to leave. He had to try and forget.

Wandering through to the kitchen, the whiskey bottle dangling loosely from his brittle fingers, he moved to the sink. He watched with a silent focus as the golden liquid drained away from the bottle, pouring out and disappearing. He could not hide in drink for the rest of his life. He had to try and accept all of the strange things that had happened here.

Aran involuntarily jumped as someone rapped on the French windows. There was a smash as he dropped the whiskey bottle. Shards of broken glass cut across the kitchen work surface. Staggering back, pained by the sudden sounds, he rubbed at his exhausted eyes.

Expecting to see the farmer's wife, although not sure why she would come here, he staggered back through to the living room and stopped in front of the closed French windows.

A man he had never seen before was waiting on the other side. The man looked tired, mentally exhausted, dragging himself through middle age by sheer will power alone. He had grey hair that had been hurriedly slicked back off his face, and equally grey saggy eyes. He was the physical embodiment of all that Aran felt at the moment. Yet this man was covered over by at the very least the façade of respectability. A bland dark grey suit, an impersonal navy blue tie hanging limply around his neck. Aran's eyes shifted to the background and was surprised to discover PC Staples stood close to a patrol car like the grim reaper. Behind the looming stature of the constable waited a WPC. She looked as though she was trying to hide her uncertainty. She was trying to be confident, strong and unbeatable. She had almost pulled it off.

Numbly reaching out, Aran unlocked the French windows.

"Aran Sellere?" the middle aged man immediately spoke. His eyes bore directly into Aran's bewildered face without a thought of apology.

Aran nodded slowly.

"DS Springs," the man introduced himself. "Mind if I have a quick word?" he asked, stepping back from the door and moving a hand through the cool early morning air. The gesture stood as an invitation. The sun light was crisp at this hour.

Aran automatically followed him out without thinking. "Of course," he said, surprised by how drained he sounded. "What's this all about?"

Springs pursed his lips, unwilling to answer straight away. Staples and the unnamed female constable moved silently to the cottage and slipped in through the French windows. "You don't mind if they have a quick look around, do you? It's just a matter of routine," the detective commented in an off hand manner, dragging Aran's attention back away from the cottage.

If he had not been hung over he would have protested. If he had not been lost in this whirlpool of grief, he would have stopped them. He knew his rights and he usually defended them with vigour. He could only presume that Patrick Knight had sent them here to collect up any remaining incriminating evidence.

But the situation was not the norm. Things had changed. He was not as strong as he once had been. This year had been hard, he had suffered, and he did not seem to be as quick as he once had been. Perhaps he did not care anymore. "Did Knight send you?"

Springs' brow wrinkled in confusion. "Knight? Do you mean Patrick Knight?" he guessed. "You know as well as I do the man died a few days ago."

"Right, of course," Aran sighed, closing his eyes for a moment. It was confusing trying to keep track of all of these parallel versions of reality. It was a struggle sometimes to remember which belonged to him. "So what is this about?"

"I see you're heading off now." Springs nodded towards the ungainly heaps of cardboard boxes, suitcases and plastic bags. "Last day in the area. Did you have a nice time yesterday? Did you get everything sorted out? It was the village fete yesterday, so I've been told. Did you manage to sample some of the local culture?"

In not knowing what was happening, he was off his guard. He could only tell the truth. He could see Springs was searching for something, the way the man set his words tentatively out into the air. "Yes, I was there for a bit."

"I've already spoken to some of the locals actually," The detective confessed. "They mentioned that they saw you there. They also mentioned seeing you heading off to the woods near by. Is that true?"

Aran nodded slowly. He had gone to the woods yesterday. He had finally done the thing he was supposed to do. He had saved her. Of course he could never explain that to the detective. He would not understand. He would never believe all the talk of dimensions, the theoretical physics, the sheer bizarre nature of this area. "I went for a walk in the woods."

Springs was a little taken aback. Perhaps he had not expected Aran to admit to it. "It's supposed to be nice walking around there. So the local land lord tells me. He mentioned that one of the other locals went off there early yesterday morning. She'd just got back into the country. Ludvine Moore is her name. She'd told the couple who run the local pub that she'd be back after an hour. She never returned. As you can imagine, they got worried so they went out to the woods in the early afternoon…"

"Sir, I…." The WPC was stood in the doorway clutching some sheets of paper.

Springs held up his hand. "Just a moment. I need to ask Mr. Sellere something." He turned his gaze back to the bewildered journalist. "Do you know Miss Moore?"

"Yes, I…" Aran faltered. Did he really know her? The girl he had known did not exist to him. She had been the product of some kind of blip in the space time continuum. The Ludvine Moore of today was someone he had first met yesterday. He had saved her life. What was he supposed to tell the detective? He could hardly explain how Patrick Knight, a man who had died of a heart attack, a man who was now residing in a morgue miles away, had attacked her in the woods. They had decided not to tell anyone about what had happened, because they would both be regarded as lunatics. Thus, he had never met her. He had already broken his promise to her.

"Interesting, because she'd only just got back into the country," Springs spoke coyly. "You know we found her, up in the woods. She wasn't hard to find. No attempt to hide the body had been made…"

"What are you talking about?" Aran interrupted. The detective couldn't say such things. He had saved Ludvine; he could remember every moment. He had not been through all this in vain. Surely she had not been foolish enough to return to the woods that very same day. Please, Ludvine, not again.

Springs misread the urgency in Aran's voice.

PC Staples stepped into the door way as the WPC moved out into the sunlight. "Sir, I found this in the bedroom."

The policeman held up one of Aran's sweaters, his fingers protected by the plastic sheen of latex gloves. As if Aran emitted some kind of poison. The sweater was heavy and crumpled. It was covered in blood. Nausea began to build in Aran's stomach. He had to be dreaming now. His eyes moved to the WPC, to the photographs she was holding. The pictures of Ludvine. Countless pictures of Ludvine. Ludvine whom he had loved.

Aran turned back to the detective. "She's dead, isn't she?"

Springs let out an exhausted sigh. "I think you made sure of that, didn't you?" As he spoke he wondered if Aran had any idea of what he had done. Either he was an excellent liar or something had gone very wrong in his mind. "Aran Sellere, I am arresting you for the murder of Ludvine Moore."

Numbness flooded his veins, the world weakening and sagging around him. That had just been a bad dream; he would never kill Ludvine. It had just been a nightmare. He had to be dreaming. Dear God, it could not all be his fault.

As he felt the cool metal of the handcuffs touch the skin around his wrists, he realised that this was not a dream. It was one of the many paths his life could have and would take. Fate was unstoppable. This really was happening.

www.ingramcontent.com/pod-product-compliance
Ingram Content Group UK Ltd.
Pitfield, Milton Keynes, MK11 3LW, UK
UKHW041438180426
11947UKWH00007B/509